BEAUTY SECRETS
of the
MARTYRS

Verity Holloway

Pippa

INVISIBLE
MILLINER

Published by Invisible Milliner 2015

invisiblemilliner.com

verityholloway.com

ISBN: 978-1-910857-00-7

A catalogue record for this book is available from the British
Library.

1

"The Church has painstakingly collected the records of those who persevered to the end in witnessing to their faith. These are the acts of the Martyrs. They form the archives of truth written in letters of blood."
— *Catechism of The Catholic Church.*

"For men to be instructed, they must be seduced by aesthetics, but how can anyone render the image of death agreeable?"
— *Arnaud Éloi Gautier-d'Agoty, anatomical illustrator (1741–1771).*

THE NEWS CHANNELS called it The Clownfish Calamity, but I knew it as Miracle from the first.

They were migrating, the scientists say. Forty-thousand orange clownfish washed ashore on England's New Southern Coast. Their reef homes gone, the waters of the tropics rusty with pollutants and unnaturally cold, they took to the unknown, casting their bodies to the whim of the tides. Brave little clowns in striped jackets, gasping and freezing on the leaden shingle.

Once we looked to earthquakes to gauge the mood of God. I mean, I've seen some sights since the fourth century... but lately things have taken a creative turn.

Oh, no flash photography, please. Alright, just one. Do it with your phone, nice and quick, at an angle so the glass doesn't glare. I'll lie still.

It's a lovely setup here, with my bower under the altar. They've put me in a swoon, throat bared, hair fanned out on the pillow. The arterial red archways soar over me, a dark-bright gilded aura in the candlelight. I look as though I am dreaming this place, my lips parted in a sigh of wonder at the gifts bestowed on me by God. If you were critical, you'd say I look like I might snore. But we're beyond such indelicacies, my type.

Be mindful of the puddles. Since the most recent big rains, the laywomen have put a sign up so nobody can chase us for money when they slip over. I think legal nastiness is really more of an American problem. Here in Croatia, especially since Egypt went under, and Sumatra, people are laid back about the small stuff. We've got high harbour walls, our yellow rocky hills. We won't be taken for a while.

Welcome to Dubrovnik. I am Silvan, and this, the Church of Saint Blaise, is my home. My place of work.

Without being too obnoxious about it, I'm a bit of a crowd-pleaser.

They come to me from across the remaining world, the pious and the curious. In their rubber boots and anoraks, their dripping wheelchairs, they approach me, thumbing plastic prayer beads, airport-bleary, thirsty for coffee and for answers. My bower beneath the altar is the opposite of a psychiatrist's couch, you might well say. I lie here, limp and full of dreams. You, the interpreter, lean into my light, hold your breath.

"Saint Silvan, intercede for America. Pray for the drowned of New Orleans, for the refugees from Florida."

Florida's gone, is it? Now I regret my lawsuit comment.

"Hail, O star of the ocean, God's own Mother blessed. Ever sinless Virgin, gate of heavenly rest."

Lord, bring back the icecaps. Tell them we're sorry.

And then, the timeworn incantation:

"Wow. Isn't he gorgeous?"

Even before my death, my face drew in the masses. As a boy in Rome, I would escort my sister Aurelia down the white steps of our villa and across town, to the forum. You remember the important things when this much time has passed: the sun on my bare toes, the breeze toying with my curls and the hem of the short tunic I wore for such errands. I remember the eyes on me; the eyes of women and the eyes of men, and of children just becoming women and men, and of slaves, and of animals, clucking and lowing and barking their praise as I passed by, two steps behind my sister. It wouldn't be proper to acknowledge such things at the time, of course. I was a good boy.

"So, Aurelia. How does it feel to be the second prettiest girl in the family?"

The laughing girls floated on by. Only that morning, our mother had chuckled at Aurelia's jealousy as the slaves braided her black hair. My own was a burnished golden mass that caught the eye.

"I will chop it off, one day," Aurelia said. "While you sleep."

"Think of the money we could make," Mother said, "with such a wig. Or selling the olive oil he scrapes from himself during his ablutions. Call it a love potion."

But Mother was not with us that morning at the forum, and when the jeering girls were gone, my sister took a sudden change of tack. As I followed her to the secluded spot under the arches where an old woman sold chickpea soup, she snatched up a rock and hurled it at me. It struck the base of my neck, here, where the gash is. It's not the same gash you're looking at now; she was a thirteen-year-old, not a bear. Aurelia only managed to graze me, though Mother still threatened to whip her for

4

it. *This* gash, if you read the sign the church staff have kindly hung to the left of the altar, came from a Roman spear.

Sv. Silvan Mučenik.

Martyr.

I'm as surprised as you are. My own people. You'd think I was leading the Roman Empire's PR campaign, what with the ensemble the Croatians have given me. Short white tunic. Swishy red cape. Nice little centurion sandals to complete the picture. I must have gone wrong somewhere. Probably the Christianity. So many of us in those early years met the sword, the tooth, or the nail. It is a thing of immeasurable loveliness to lay down one's life for one's faith. Look, for instance, at me.

Oh, yes. I am Miracle.

They call me 'incorrupt'. Since the day I died so many handfuls of centuries ago, not one atom of my body has succumbed to the natural way of the flesh. I never stiffened. I never grew pale. Mortals have their stern reality, of course, or think they do. All flesh is grass, and beauty like the flower in the field? No. Not if God wills it.

There is one last visitor before the church shuts for the night. She's a grown woman with the reedy body of a girl, face pale as daylight on a puddle. She comes to the altar in her trainers and stands there, dripping and staring, the way they all do. I like her immediately.

"Saint Silvan," she says. Her voice is like one of those extraordinary darting finches you used to see in the springtime. I wonder if she knows that. She gets onto her knees and shuffles close to my bower of red velvet. I see she is wearing a man's chequered shirt and a baggy Disney sweater, frayed about the cuffs. Donated clothes.

She has come from one of the shelters.

She presses her wallet to the glass. I see a photograph through my eyelashes. A husband, presumably, standing out in a field with a hoe. One of the unfortunate farmers. They feel responsible, with their blighted crops and their empty cowsheds. They see the starvation and think they recognise their own failings.

"Blessed martyr," she says, in that wondrous voice. "He's all but given up. He doesn't rise from his cot. He takes the food they give him and leaves it for the cats. Please, Silvan, hear me. He's lost everyone since the rains came. Everyone but me, and I know I'm not much to have left. We had some land. We called it The Hermitage. There were ten of us to begin with, and by the end, almost a thousand. We wanted to prove it could work again – people caring for each other. We had doctors and teachers, a bit of solar power. Everyone did their bit. I know it sounds trivial now. People heard about us and came to hear me give my little speeches about over-fishing and perishable plastics. And it was all going so well. But then the police came and read the Riot Act on us and we scattered like–" Here, she pauses to bite at her flaky upper lip. "Look, I know we'll never see our home again. I know. But what I want... what I humbly beseech you for..."

Whatever she wants, it is too much to say out loud, and instead of speaking she takes me in; the drowsing length of my body on this princely funeral bed. It soothes her, the sight of my body, lifeless yet deathless also. Her fingers curl around the gilded bars.

"I keep thinking about those clownfish. It's a sign, isn't it? It isn't like when the rhinos died out or when the wheat went funny in Poland and everyone saw scarecrows flying over Warsaw. I keep thinking of those fish lying there on the beaches. And then I look around me at the cots and the rations, and all the people. The different kinds of people. There's a banker and his wife who got there in a pleasure yacht. 'The Jolly Jamaican', moored outside like a massive joke. But at night I think of those absurd little fish crossing the ocean, and I–" She stops there. Her forehead clunks against the glass and we are within a breath of one another. "God," she sighs, as though it pains her. "You're so lovely."

Shelter Girl takes her wallet and wanders back out into the darkening streets. The laywomen close the doors and lock them, and make their rounds of the church, snuffing candles, lacing the air with smoke. I see the unspoken words of Shelter Girl like those of every other visitor before her, through famine and missile crisis, pestilence and rebellion, these past few hundred years.

If this is the end of the world, they want to know, *will you tell us?*

PLEASE EXCUSE ME while I gather my things. If I dawdle, I will never make all my appointments.

I love Cryptspace this time of year. That smell is roses. It's always roses, but in mid-spring it's 'The Generous Gardener', a coral bloom with a signature of myrrh and musk. It's a disease-resistant variety, hard to kill. Little funereal joke, there.

You can't get lost down here. Since the big rains came, you just follow the stream and enjoy the paintings. We've just acquired Delaroche's *The Young Martyr*, that haloed drowning beauty. We've hung her between Slingeneyer's *A Christian Martyr in the Reign of Diocletian* and Doré's angels flocking over the ruined bodies in the Colosseum. Very affecting with the trickle of the water and the light fluttering against the red brick. I fight the temptation to adapt these languorous poses for my purpose, for one cannot dwell on what one is forbidden to do. Imagine if I moved. Imagine the tourists. All that litter.

Cryptspace opens at dusk and closes at dawn. During opening hours, one can visit any church, catacomb, or ossuary one pleases, anywhere in the remaining world, in a fraction of the time it would take to hop on a plane. Providing one is dead. The living will find nothing down here but a basement and relief from the humidity. I can sympathise. Croatia is a terracotta Balkan heaven – or was, before – but the heat doesn't half mess with one's hair.

Johann is waiting in his galoshes. A former monk, he takes care of the gate between Saint Blaise's and the rest of Cryptspace. Johann succumbed to smallpox half a millennium after I met with blessed martyrdom, and although his flesh has been restored in death, he is still sensitive when it comes to his face, huddling there in his roughspun robe with his headphones on, like a bashful teenager. My wheeled suitcase is heavy with ointments and salves, but I would never wound him by trying to sell him any. His shyness makes him beautiful.

"What are you listening to?" I have to raise my voice for him to hear me above the headphones' tinny din.

He pulls them out. "Your supplier left a message. Expect a visit before morning."

I point again at his headphones. "Is it Mussorgsky tonight, or Sinatra?"

"Oh. Oh, it's silly," he says, tucking the little device up his sleeve. "You wouldn't like it."

I let him open the gate for me and my suitcase. It's a short stroll to France, up a flight of slippery stairs beside a waterfall foaming with green moss. A nun lets me through the gate, under an arch of blue and violet glass. She giggles as I pass. I should set her up with Johann.

My first client waits for me on the lid of her glass sarcophagus, stockinged feet swinging. Despite the dowdy nun's habit, her smooth pink face looks not a day over twenty. Though she was, I believe, thirty when she died. 1879 – practically five minutes ago.

"Have you got it?" Bernadette says excitedly.

"Pearlescent Babydoll polish in 'Peachy Keen'. There was a promotion on cuticle oil, so I picked you up a bottle. No charge."

She unscrews the cap and tests the modest rosy polish on her thumbnail. "It smells like violets!"

"They can do that now."

"I remember when it stank of acetate and I would spend all night worrying the visitors would smell it on me in the morning. It is beautiful, Silvan. I must tell Thérèse."

I do enjoy her enthusiasm. These Victorian ones can lean towards the morbid. Saint Thérèse of Lisieux once chased me from her basilica, accusing me of being an emissary of the Dark One. I only made a delicate constructive comment on her tubercular pallor, but she threw a shoe at me and called me a dirty Roman peddler of vanity. 'Little Flower' indeed. I still leave her catalogues. Really gets up her nose.

We sit together on her sarcophagus. Little peasant Bernadette, the miller's daughter turned mystic. The nuns have done very little to her over the years. She admits to some work in the 1920s to mask minimal discolouration to her face and hands, probably the fault of candle fumes, but other than that, she is internally sound and continues to inspire devotion from hundreds of visitors per day, here and at Lourdes where she first had her vision of The Virgin. Each in their own way, the pilgrims tell her she is beautiful, yet it has never gone to her head. She's the real thing.

"I've been praying for you," she says, painting her

nails. "Trotting about with your bag of wonders."

"I see saints all over the world, every week." I show her the latest catalogue. *'Breathing new life into age-old faith'*, it says, over an airbrushed photograph of a weeping Madonna. "I've had two-thousand years of lying down, gathering dust. Finally, I feel I am earning my keep."

"Did I not say you had a talent? Is this your list of appointments?"

"You are at the top, Bernadette."

"Flatterer." She nudges me, with a saucy look. "You are a man of the cloth, remember."

"Am I?"

"Look at your tunic."

It is very fine, whatever it denotes. Embroidered filigree around my bloodied neck, and a cross of gold thread studded with rubies above my heart. Whatever the content of my life after Aurelia threw that rock at me, it is safe to assume I was not a farmer, like Shelter Girl's unfortunate husband.

"Who is this?" Bernadette points to a name at the bottom of my list. "Is he newly canonised?"

"I rather doubt he will ever be canonised, Bernadette."

"But he is incorrupt?"

"Along those lines."

"Then I shall pray for him. And I will not delay you. God bless you and keep you, *mon petit*."

I pack up my things and hop down the steps into the fragrant alleys of Cryptspace.

I SURFACE IN Germany's Weyarn. My Latin soul wilts in the shadow of Bavarian Gothic ramparts. But I have come to see my friends Valerius and Deodatus.

Saint Deodatus has come all the way from Roggenburg tonight. Or rather, Valerius has fetched him from Roggenburg, because when you are a skull on a velvet cushion, your travel options are somewhat limited.

As I climb up into the dark nave, the teasing begins.

"Avon calling. The Bishop of Thessaloniki is here with your potions, Val."

"Silvan!"

Saint Valerius has a voice like splitting oak and dashes about on his toes, like a raptor. He clambers down from his golden bower and treats me to one of his stony embraces, squeezing the air from my incorrupt lungs. I was afraid of him at first, being so tall and nought but bone, but I have come to see Valerius as proof that one's heart is more than a mere muscle in one's chest.

They do things splendidly in this region. Valerius' skeleton is dressed exclusively in jewels. His moustache is a cluster of diamonds and his eyes sapphires that glint with humour and dignity. A crown of golden filigree and a spray of palm fronds – the badge of one who has bled for Christ – complete his magnificence. He nudges my cheeks with his glittering teeth. He'd like to kiss, but what can you do?

"You look well, my boy," he says. "So bronzed."

I go to Deodatus' cushion. He likes to pretend his face is beyond all earthly intervention, so I've learnt to indulge his air of amused disdain while taking his orders.

"What did you just call me?" I ask him.

Deodatus grunts as I lean down to kiss his crown of gilded emeralds. "The Bishop of Thessaloniki. Christ on a bike. He's forgotten again."

Valerius places both bony hands on my shoulders and grins down at me.

"The holy, glorious, all-laudable Apostle Silvan underwent many sorrows and misfortunes for the Lord's sake. After suffering much he entered the repose of the Blessed."

He prods the wound in my neck. Air escapes with a whistling noise. "That sounds impressive. Do you think they could put that on my sign?"

"Why don't you ask them?" Deodatus sniggers. He is, of course, right. Talk about the end of the world – we, the walking dead! No, our night-time excursions are ours alone.

I unpack their orders. Two tubes of whitening toothpaste, a can of Brasso with a chamois cloth, and, for Valerius, a bottle of gentleman's cologne. It smells of leather and grave dirt and is a great favourite among the heavy metal boys and girls who flock to see him each week, despite their parents' warnings about death cults and extremism and the erosion of modern enlightenment. He dabs a little onto his collarbones and sighs.

Deodatus allows me to buff his crown with Brasso. "So, Your Holiness, are the rumours true? Your appointment later. I heard worrying things."

I frown. "From who?"

"A little flower told me."

Thérèse of Lisieux. I've only brought it upon myself.

"Silvan is perfectly entitled to do as he pleases," Valerius says. "There is nothing in the rules to say who — or what — he may sell to. Come to think of it, I am not aware of any rules at all."

"Don't get the hump with Thérèse," Deodatus says. "We talk — what else are we expected to do all night? Anyway, I want to know what he's ordered."

I chuckle at his impertinence.

"Ideologically opposed is what I thought he'd be," he says. "Not to mention, you haven't dressed sensibly for the journey."

"This is all I have," I say, tugging my tunic down my thighs. "I don't feel the cold."

"When your lot invaded Northern Europe, you know what the Roman army had their women knit? *Foot mittens*. Little forked foot mittens to go under sandals. Not good boots for soggy English soil, not oilskins for drizzly winters. Foot mittens. No wonder they sodded off home again. You hate to adapt, that's your problem. It's Rome's way, or no way at all, and look where that got *you*."

"I thought I was Greek."

"You were the *bishop* of a Greek *diocese*, not an actual bloody *Greek*. Has your miraculous brain finally shrivelled up?"

Valerius raises Deodatus to face-height as if he were a small, impudent dog. "Have we not talked about the counting to ten before the opening of the mouth, little friend?"

"It's a good job he's pretty, that's all I'm saying."

"Pay him no mind, my boy. Allow me to settle my account." Valerius prises a ruby from his ribs and presses it into my palm. "I would advise – if you will permit me to do so, bishop – a little caution tonight. Will you promise me to leave if things become, shall we say, confrontational?"

Deodatus hoots. "It's not like you can exsanguinate twice."

"I do not anticipate violence," Valerius says. "But this is odd, Silvan."

I shrug. "We cannot be afraid of people simply because they are not Christian."

"Quite right."

"And I expect he'll be charming."

"Let us not stretch credulity." Valerius puts his hand on my head, smoothing my hair. "That such a man would reach out to us strikes me as improbable, if not impossible. If something happens, Silvan... you know you may call for my aid."

"Not mine?" says Deodatus, affronted despite having no intention of helping whatsoever.

"You don't have limbs," Valerius says.

I pat Deodatus' crown. "It's true. You don't. But you needn't worry. The impossible is simply what I do."

My FINAL APPOINTMENT is not for another hour, so I cross back over to France to have a word with Thérèse of Lisieux. The Little Flower of Jesus has never been much of a sociable creature, and I find her reclining amid golden opulence with her crown of white roses, seemingly asleep.

Don't mistake this pretty sight for Thérèse's mortal shell. When Thérèse was dying of tuberculosis in 1897, one of her fellow nuns suggested that her life of love and trust in the Lord would make her a candidate for the perfect preservation of the flesh. Thérèse put her meek little hands together and chirped, "Oh no. Not that miracle." She was right. Upon exhumation, Thérèse's body had gone the way of all − or most − flesh, and the sweet snoozing saint I view now is a mere model. Hence, unlike myself and my friends, she rarely gets up to stretch her legs.

Still, she can't stand me, and I am no more than six feet into the chapel before she opens her eyes.

"My vocation is love, and love alone. You can take

your greasepaint and get out."

"I'm not here to sell you anything. In fact, I would like my catalogues back." It's pure cheek, and I will make my amends later, but riling her up is a temptation I cannot quite resist.

She sits up, adjusting her crown of roses. "I have recycled them all."

"Isn't it a little late to be worrying about landfill?" I scuff at the stones with my sandal. "Anyway, Deodatus said you were quite taken with Yardley's floral talcum powder."

"Don't you have somewhere to be?"

"I do. In fact, I do. As well you know."

"I am appalled," she says. "Everyone is."

"Isn't gossip a sin?"

"Freedom of information. It will be a human right one day, Silvan, and you can take that from one who talks to the upper management."

This piques my interest. Archangels, The Powers, Ascended Apostles. Being that I was little more than a boy when I died, I retain that puppyish curiosity for my unseen betters. "Do they talk about me?"

Thérèse bares her teeth. "Van-it-y."

"You deliberately misunderstand," I say. Now it is I who is riled. "My work is producing wonderful results. An eight-year-old girl was taken by her parents to see Bernadette last week, and you know what she said? 'Mama, she is beautiful. God must love her very much'. And her Mummy replied, 'And He loves you just as much, my darling'. It was perfect. The stuff of a morality play."

"And your nail polish is to thank for that touching moment?"

"Beauty leaves an impression."

"Then why visit that horrid old man?"

"I feel I might do some good."

She kicks open her gleaming sarcophagus and climbs out. "I can hear the pilgrims now. 'Mummy, our glorious leader looks so beautiful. The State must love him very much'."

I glower at the flagstones. I have never been good with sharp-witted women.

"You are not the right candidate for this," she says. "I don't think anyone is."

"I'm ideal. I'm friendly. I know which colours suit which complexions. People like me. When they visit me in Dubrovnik, they are always saying how lovely I am, how well-preserved, and the distraction is good for them. They need a place where the rain can't—" My voice has risen to an adolescent whine, and I gather myself. "Where it can't touch them."

We stare at each other, listening to the wind assailing the lead-veined windows.

"Be that as it may," she says. "I tell you this lovingly, and without judgement: You're thick, Silvan. You are suited to pedalling meaningless powders and paints, and I admit they may do no harm, but this – this *thing* you are set on doing – is so beyond you, it frightens me."

The rain has started up again. I think of my sister, Aurelia, making me run her errands in the wet weather while she lounged on her couch, complaining of headaches. I have always been useful and intend to remain so.

I take my suitcase of dirty Roman vanity and turn back to Cryptspace. Thérèse calls to me, something French and apologetic. I stride on to colder climes.

18

ALRIGHT, YES, MAYBE I dressed inappropriately. Even the stones of Cryptspace can't fend off the cruelty of the rain in these Eastern lands, and my cloak is barely suited to protecting the skin from the sun. The leaks in the vaulted ceiling are so numerous, water lashes down onto my head in a continuous spray. No wonder the Roman Empire backed off and let the Huns have Russia. The heathens are welcome to it.

"I, ah… have an appointment."

At first, the guard just stares. He is no monk. He has a beard like a swarm of black bees and ferocious eyes. He'd look beautiful with some kohl, and when I tell him so, he raises one eyebrow and unlocks the gate.

"Thank you. Thanks awfully."

I have to climb up through a hatch. The guard wordlessly passes my suitcase to me from below. He is smirking. Perhaps he can see up my tunic.

Well, this is different.

What a lot of granite. How black and how red. Even the jagged red banners are made of stone. Not a Gothic

19

arch to be seen, no candles, not so much as a sliver of stained glass. I understand Russian customs to be more austere than our own, but this? I let my suitcase topple over as I take the mausoleum in. It is terribly cold, in every sense, and I totter about, taking in the height of the place and its crystalline, sterile air, until I stumble backwards into the angular glass sarcophagus. My gasp betrays my nervousness.

"Don't worry. It's bulletproof."

The sarcophagus is empty. My client has already climbed out to greet me, and I am wholly unprepared, for when I turn to see him standing there, I do the rudest thing one can do to the dead – I squeak in fright.

He is green.

He is wearing a black suit and tie, and is nearly bald, with a neat moustache and goatee of fair hair. His hands are clenched into fists at his sides, but his face is passive. And green. Hilariously, dreadfully pea soup green where the cheeks stretch hollow over bone. What paint could possibly coax life back into those cheeks, let alone beauty? It's an unkind thought, one I will pay penance for later, but…

Perhaps I shouldn't have come.

"Mister Lenin. Hello. Forgive me. How nice to meet you at last."

"My appearance does not please you."

"It isn't your fault. You aren't incorrupt." It is meant to be polite, but one side of his crisp moustache quirks, and I see I have offended him. "I apologise, sir. You just aren't touched by divinity… in that particular way."

"I am not touched by divinity at all."

"Don't give up hope, Mister Lenin." I try to smile. I cannot read his expression as he steps towards me, taking in my filigree finery. I look flimsy against all this uncompromising granite.

"What is… all this… about?" he asks.

"My outfit?" I am instantly relieved, and give him a twirl. "The Croatians gave me this. I was on display in Rome until 1847, but then someone saw fit to move me. I don't recall why. But this costume is ideal for the Croatian climate, even now. Do you like my sandals?"

He doesn't say. I am not yet used to the cold. My flesh in its perfection does not pucker, but he notices nonetheless.

"The Mediterranean has made you soft," he says, as if some long-held prejudice has been confirmed. "I would offer you comfort, but alas, a low temperature is necessary in this room, as I am not touched – as you put it – by divinity."

He comes closer to pick up my fallen suitcase. He moves stiffly, and when he bends, I marvel at his figure.

"Gosh, sir. Aren't you thin."

"My keepers removed my internal organs."

Oh. That was very Egyptian of them. I half expect to see a row of canopic jars on a shelf somewhere, bearing the red hammer and sickle.

"You wonder why? How little you know of mortal men, Silvan. I am no miracle. You, on the other hand…" One green fist uncurls with a crackle of bone to rest upon my chest. "You inspire wonder in your followers."

I am compelled to look away. "They are the Lord's followers, sir. I am simply a vessel."

"A vessel. You are intact, aren't you?"

He taps on my breastbone. I sound like a hollow log.

He regards me for a moment longer with his intelligent eyes, then bids me sit with him on the marble

21

lip of his open sarcophagus. "Your employers told me of your skill at transforming mere flesh into inspirational loveliness."

I do wish he wouldn't sound so cynical about it. "Well, I don't really have employers. I order products wholesale from the catalogue, then sell them to martyrs and… people like yourself. I am a free agent."

"You mean to say God Almighty is not involved?"

"He is involved in everything. Every infinitesimal thing. The grass, the breeze, the—"

"Rain?"

He has cut the thread of my thought. "I focus on what I'm good at."

"Which is…?" He is inspecting the contents of my suitcase. I can hardly tell him to stop, but when he discovers the bikini wax, I am distinctly uncomfortable.

"That isn't for you."

"I imagine not."

"I've taken the liberty of picking out some samples I thought you might enjoy. I am meeting with my supplier this morning and can order anything that takes your fancy right away. I recommend these mineral powders for the cheeks and brow – they reflect the light softly, like a heavenly glow."

He glances my way. "Do I want to appear heavenly?"

"'Radiant' is another, equally apt word."

"The radiant Vladimir Lenin." He takes the pot of powder from me with his green hand and examines it. I see now that his body relies on the golden lights embedded inside his sarcophagus to soften the amphibious tone of his skin. I am about to suggest an ingenious bronzer by a Parisian institute of cosmetics when I notice his glass eyes have swivelled towards me.

"How old were you when you died?" he asks.

"Why, I don't know." It was such a long time ago. You really do stop counting the candles on the cake. In my case, I have forgotten the taste of cake altogether.

"I was fifty-three," he tells me. "Following the soldiers' revolution, the storming of the winter palace, and the famine and the struggle, I suffered three strokes. Attempts on my life had left me weak. I retained a bullet in my neck – yes, not unlike your own little wound there – though a surgeon did the best he could to remove it. I needed to speak, to orate with vigour! But within a year, my time had come. My funeral was an occasion of glorious public grief. Over five days, three quarters of a million of my countrymen braved the winter to view my body in state. Since my preservation, hundreds of millions have come from every country on Earth to look upon my remains and ponder my life's work. All this was done with none of your dirty religious artifice."

His eyes are alight with fervour. He looks almost alive. "How beautiful to be so loved."

It is not the reaction he is hoping for. "I may not be pretty, young man, but my devotion to the revolution raised the powerless up from their knees. Some say I was too violent. That my belief in the betterment of the serfs was even comical in its vehemence. I taught my followers to hurl acid at policemen. I took bullets to the chest. I denied myself everything I took pleasure in for fear of it softening my heart. Even music. Beethoven. But you? You here, with your girl's clothes and your soft hands? What have you done to deserve the admiration of those who lay eyes upon your remains?"

He stares at me, full of expectation, and, I realise, triumph. My fingers trace the gash in my neck. I had not prepared myself for an interview. I could lie to him; say my martyrdom was a grand and terrible affair in the baking heat of Rome. That I was dragged to the Colosseum beneath the glare of screaming crowds, and refused to recant my faith or even make a sound of pain as my body succumbed to the artistry of Roman torture. He would appreciate that, I think.

But I am a saint, and we have a duty not to lie.

"Answer me," he commands. "What was your life, before all of this?"

"I lived in Rome. And perhaps Greece, for a time. Valerius said…" I shake my head. "I'm not sure. I will have to ask him again. Or Deodatus might know."

"Who is Deodatus?"

"The jewelled skull of Saint Deodatus of…" He has edged closer without my realising it. His critical look flusters me. "Deodatus of… somewhere. A martyr. He is said to have raised the Eastern provinces of Anglia from unhappy unrighteousness. Which is funny, really, when you meet him. He is something of a sourpuss."

"No further citations?"

This insistence on detail is most unusual. "I think he was put to death sometime in the sixth century. Perhaps the seventh. He will yell at me if I ask, but if you'd like him to dredge up nasty memories…"

"I don't care for dry bones," Lenin says. "I would like to know more about you. When did you die, precisely?"

"The fourth century."

"I said precisely."

"Precisely sometime in the fourth century. It might say on my sign."

"And, for you, decomposition was optional?"

"I am intact as a testament to God's mysteries."

A smirk. "You seem to have had a little help since the fourth century. Is that wax I see, coating your boyish face?"

"Vaseline moisturiser. I was expecting the cold to chap me something dreadful, so I popped by the Ukraine to apply some on the way."

"And I suppose those lips are like roses thanks to your... what did you modestly call it? 'Divinity'?"

I shake my head. "Revlon's Cherries In The Snow. Pretty name."

"This is interesting to me. You consciously take part in the artifice of your preservation, yet believe your own lies."

"Oh, they aren't lies." I take a catalogue from my suitcase and show him the slogan on the cover: *Breathing new life into age-old faith*. The phrase triggers a memory. "Hang on. Yes. I was a bishop. I must have been martyred for turning my back on the Roman gods. Isn't that lovely?"

"Do you think they make bishops as young as you?"

"I have always had a youthful appearance."

He huffs at this. "You say you 'must have been' martyred. Do you not remember?"

I remember rain. But then, it has been raining for years. Only the sea defences saved Dubrovnik from a fate like Venice's. Deodatus' Eastern provinces of England were some of the first to go, and I have tried not to be upset by news of my own Rome, its seven hills a collection of muddy slopes rolling down into a quagmire. They used to call these disasters acts of God. There are still mortal men claiming none of this was their fault. Big American cars. Passenger jets. Chugging factories. Not a fair trade for all those lost lands and dislocated souls.

Lenin awaits my answer.

"It has been many hundreds of years, and I cannot remember my life as a bishop," I admit. "But I am wearing priestly clothes, am I not?"

"If I painted my nose red, would that make me a clown?"

"It would make you quite frightening."

He laughs at this. It must have been a hearty laugh in life, before his chest was emptied of matter. "The little lamb of God is so easily startled."

Is he flirting with me? I'm not sure that's appropriate.

"Listen, little lamb," he says. "I will take your powders and whatever else you offer me, though I cannot say I will use them. All I ask is that you return, and soon. I would like to speak with you at leisure, about a great many things."

"I would be only too glad," I say. It is a lie the size of Russia.

I RETURN TO Dubrovnik before the dawn. Johann greets me, tugging the earphones from his tonsured head.

"How did it go?"

"Don't tell me you've been listening to Thérèse's gossip."

"Oh, no. Only music. Your visitor is upstairs. I told them it was alright to wait."

"Them?"

He tucks his brown sleeves over his hands and shrugs. "You'll see."

It is a woman. A mannish woman, I think as I tug my suitcase towards my altar where the figure waits, leaning on a column. It could be a womanish man, on reflection. Whatever they are, they have a lovely bottom in suit trousers and a jaunty way of swinging around to wave at me, like a character in one of those black and white entertainment films I've caught a few minutes of, here and there, these past few hundred years.

"Here he is!" my visitor cries. "I was beginning to take roots. Say, d'you know someone left their wallet under a

27

pew over there? Two-hundred Kuna. I'd suggest we pop out to a pub, but it's a bit late, and you're dead. I'm Az, by the way. Pleasure to meet you at last."

He or she kisses both my cheeks twice. Pink flesh and warm hands; a relief after Lenin.

"What are your preferred pronouns, Az?" I ask. That is the polite thing to do these days.

"I could ask you the same. You could pass as anything, pretty face like that." Az winks. The flirting is less creepy than Mister Lenin's, and I smile. "Male? Then we shall be male together."

Az gives a shake of his tail feathers and if I'm not mistaken, the width of his hips decreases and he gains a few inches in height, making us eye-to-eye. He's wearing a striped seersucker blazer and a pink tie suggestive of lemonade picnics by English rivers in a bygone age. I see he has brought me a selection of new products. Waterproof mascaras. As if anyone could get away with the other variety these days.

"I take it this is the first time you've met one of us in person," he says, shaking out his cuffs.

"It is. The products have a way of simply arriving. I'm not complaining, you understand. It's nice to see a new face."

"You've been doing so well, we thought it high time we sent someone to congratulate you. Truth be told, I was expecting someone less impressive. You hear all sorts about incorrupt bodies, and it's usually some desiccated old Mother Superior with three teeth." He bites his lip, pretending to belatedly realise he is bad-mouthing the Church within a holy sanctuary. "Your teeth are splendid, though. As is your work. Everyone's talking about you. Up there, down below, all over the show."

"Down… below?"

He grins, baring gums the colour of cold pink gin. He makes a vague 'circling-the-drain' motion with his finger and I realise with a twinge of concern what manner of creature I am speaking to.

At least Thérèse isn't here to see it.

"Come now," Az chuckles. "Don't pull that face. Community service, old boy! Everyone's got a right to improve himself, even at this late stage. It's sort of a joke, anyway. Eternity in Hell with the legions of the Fallen, or a job in retail. Decisions, decisions."

Az isn't human. I know humans. That leaves one possibility. I watch him saunter to the altar and inspect the bottoms of the candlesticks for hallmarks. Angels in their unadulterated form – though I have never seen such a wonder – are many-headed flaming beasts, messengers of blinding light and beauty so entire, it leaves one shaking. Az still has puppy fat.

I can't help it. With his smiling eyes and jaunty step, he is so very comely. Fallen or otherwise, I like him.

"Besides…" he says. "You were a Roman. If we could project your life onto the wall right now, it'd be: *Orgy, vomiting, orgy, thrown to the lions…*"

"Was I thrown to lions?"

"You've got that big gash. I don't know. Have you considered Googling yourself?"

"Valerius says the Internet is the Devil's petri dish."

Az raises an eyebrow. "Do you know what a petri dish is?"

"Something bad."

He drums on the altar. "How'd your last appointment go? Bit of a curve-ball, eh?"

"It was… interesting."

"Interesting like *ooooh* or like *aaaargh?*"

"A little of both," I admit. Before I can stop myself, I whisper, "He's *green.*"

"Green? Gosh. Anyway, frightfully Christian of you to do it. Judge not, et cetera. And if anyone's qualified to make someone a little less green, it's you. With your track record, you'll have tiny Russian children holding hands and singing their praises to Uncle Vlad's rosy cheeks in no time. That's what beauty's all about, isn't it? Pleasing other people."

Is it? He makes it sound like servitude. "I find cosmetics please the wearer most of all. They encourage confidence to come to the fore. Like a talisman. Or warpaint."

"Ooh, a war?" he says. "I like that."

I have never been good at expressing myself. An icon of the Archangel Michael catches my attention. Serene of eye, he pierces the Devil with a spear. "A way of strengthening oneself," I say. "Opening the inner core of loveliness. That takes bravery."

Az is pleased with me. He leans back, elbows on the altar. "Strength. War. You're so philosophical, Silvan. Maybe you picked that up in Greece. Hey, how's about I strengthen myself right now? Your swords-and-sandals getup is so nifty, I have to try it. Hold tight."

He takes a long breath, as if preparing to dive into deep water. I expect a chant in Tongues, a theatrical flourish, but Az merely puts his hands to his face and rearranges his hair. I barely notice him changing at all, even as the striped blazer ignites into a bright metal breastplate, and then –

"Oh. Oh, goodness. No."

"You don't like it?"

I back away from the altar and drop into one of the pews in the front row, looking up at him. I have never met a creature like him before. I am not a mystic, like Bernadette. My realm is the Earth. I am a static thing, an unnatural body full of *now, now, now.* My realm, I tell myself as if it will chase away my fear, is not the past.

"Turn back," I say. "Please."

This creature before me pouts. "You'll hurt my feelings."

How tall he has become. How long and thick his legs in that soldier's kilt. Proud tapestry of scars, a map of all those straight Roman roads slicing the planet. Golden skin, close-cropped hair as black as a dog of war, and…

One thumb missing.

I turn my face to the red walls of the church. "Please change back, Az. I liked how you were before."

This large man blinks back at me, expressionless all but a hint of a smile on his lips. They are chapped by the sun. They always were. And that glistening thumb. Oh, heavens, it hasn't even healed.

"Am I not handsome, Silvan?"

I cannot lie. "Beautiful. But please—"

"As you wish. Fusspot."

Az slithers back into his more boyish form, each slight swell of his softening body chasing away the fear that seized me so inexplicably. Did I know that man? My hands shake. When it is over, Az puts his thumb to his lips, whole again, and sucks on the tip.

"Say, listen to that," he says. "It's stopped raining."

AURELIA ONCE TOLD me that if it weren't for my face, she would replace me with one of the African monkeys that danced for coins in the forum. A monkey could have lived my life, true enough. When we were children together, she daily had me carry her playthings from room to room, walking behind her like a procession after a queen. I would bring her fruit to eat, and scoop up the family cats for her to cuddle. They always ran from her. When she became a woman – I can see her now, in a rare flood of memory, a dark-haired small thing so different to me with my fair curls – the habit was too ingrained to quit, and I trotted behind her, almost a grown man, catering to this tiny woman's every desire. I didn't dislike it, though I objected to her throwing wet fruit pits at me to see if they would stick to my hair. Once, when she slapped my face for watching the pretty girls in town, I called her a spoiled little savage. Our mother beat me for raising my voice so, then beat Aurelia for mistreating me. There were many beatings, I recall. I wish I could remember something pleasant.

The night after my meeting with Mister Lenin, I catch Johann the monk resting down in Cryptspace. His head is tilted back against the wall as he listens to his music, eyes closed in bliss. I have my suitcase with me, ready for another night of appointments, and I trundle right up to him before he notices and stumbles to his feet, cowl akimbo.

"You gave me a shock. I was on another planet."

"It's lovely to see you so content. Is that for me?" I point at the origami rose on the wet flagstones.

"Oh, indeed. A letter. Thérèse of Liseux had it sent up yesterday, but by the time I received it, you'd already settled back under the altar and I didn't want to disturb you."

He passes me the rose. I unfold it.

Well? What happened? Come and tell me the damage.

"Shall I send a reply?" Johann asks.

I consider sending him off with an origami middle finger, but that's probably Az's influence talking.

"I'll save her interrogation for later. I must make my way to Russia first."

Johann's brow wrinkles. "Him again?"

"It isn't so bad. I've borrowed a thermal vest for the occasion."

"I don't understand how he ended up on your list. You've never sold to anyone outside the Church before. And him in particular..." He leans in to offer a confidence. "I saw a documentary once. They say he laid the foundations for Stalin's terrible purges. It was like the Inquisition all over again, and you know what upper management thinks of that."

"I am certain management have their reasons. And besides, Mister Az says his involvement is community service. Perhaps I am a social worker now. Perhaps my job is to help Mister Lenin see the light."

"Better you than me, Silvan. But then, that is why you were a bishop and I nothing but a monk."

"My *favourite* monk," I tell him, and he grins at his sandals, popping his headphones back into his ears. "And you never did tell me what you were listening to."

"Perhaps I will play you some, later."

LENIN WAITS ON the edge of his bulletproof sarcophagus. Still green, still thin, still not smiling.

"I have been studying your Catholic Church. Its many foibles are fascinating to me."

Most people say 'hello'. I imagine him alive, with blood in his cheeks and coastal wind in his hair. I wonder how I might bring that back. Contouring, perhaps, with blusher, and a bit of oily conditioning spray; something salty and evocative of beautiful soaring ships. But who wants to be reminded of the sea?

So instead, I say: "That's wonderful! Did you have anything in particular you wish to discuss?"

"Many things. More than I think you would have the patience for. Sit, Silvan. Let me look at you."

I settle down beside him. I think of Johann and his talk of abysmal Russian purges, but I see nothing more than a balding man before me, a man who wants to talk, and I cannot reconcile those clashing images. I know little of Mister Lenin's dreams of a classless society, but still I am mystified by how such a noble goal can come to

35

dousing policemen with acid, as he boasted. Mortal men do seem to love their extremes. Perhaps they are bored.

"Consider the case of Padre Pio," he tells me. "A Capuchin friar in the early twentieth century, he claimed to possess wounds on his body corresponding with the wounds of Jesus Christ; a painful bleeding from the palms, where Roman nails hung him on the cross. These wounds gave off a scent of flowers; the odour of sanctity, they call it, yes? As if bleeding palms were not enough, Padre Pio reportedly began to exhibit supernatural powers of healing and prophecy. Even levitation. A regular magician, with worldwide fame. For fifty years, those wounds remained. That is, until his death, when his body was found to be unblemished. Not so much as a pinprick."

"Yes, a humbling story. He was canonised by the late John Paul II, not so long ago."

"Despite the evidence? Despite the carbolic acid he used to bring up red spots on his palms, to prolong his fame and influence when investigators came to call? I would have thought such allegations would be considered most seriously before taking the drastic step of deifying—"

"Canonising."

"I don't care what you call it. Explain."

"Well, I never met him. I'm sure he was lovely."

His eyebrows come together in an expression of singular annoyance. "Loveliness doesn't come into it. Do you want to know what else I discovered? His gym sock."

"His gym sock?"

"Padre Pio's gym sock is on display for pilgrims to venerate."

I nod.

"His gym sock."

"His *venerable* gym sock."

He throws up his hands. "Surely you agree that is ridiculous."

"I have never seen the sock in question. Perhaps if I did, I would experience intense spiritual joy. I don't know."

"Intense spiritual joy. At the sight of a priest's used sock."

"I have seen God's glory in the strangest places, Mister Lenin. I have seen it in nutshells rolling by a refuse bin. I have seen it in the pigeons of Dubrovnik when they stray inside my church. I have even felt my eyes well up with love at the echo of a woman's sneeze as she stood before me at the altar. She was so apologetic. As if she had any control over her nose. Sweet lady."

"Then why, if God's glory can so effortlessly be discerned in the daily tug-and-grind of a peasant's life, do you bother gilding your great churches? Why do you take the trouble to do what you do, lying there, day after day, when a gym sock is perfectly adequate for the purpose?"

"Everyone must be catered to, Mister Lenin. One imagination is never the same as the next. We strive to spark wonder in the hearts of all. It wouldn't do to leave anyone out."

He huffs. "Anyone, for instance, too wrapped up in material greed to notice anything that isn't gold?"

"That is a little unkind. Children love bright colours, do they not?"

"Children. Yes, we agree on one point. But there is one more thing I wish to discuss with you. Admittedly, my studies have not been exhaustive, and my resources here are limited, but I was disappointed not to find any information about you, Silvan. Certainly, I found a number of holy men with your name. A Silvanus, a Sylvan, and so on, and some vague talk of glorious martyrdom at the hands of – perhaps – the Roman Empire, but beyond that…" He spreads his green hands.

"I was a bishop," I tell him as assuredly as I may. "I suffered greatly and then reposed in the Lord some two-thousand years ago. God chose to preserve me in the bloom of youth, so that my appearance may inspire wonder in all those who look upon me."

"Much like a gym sock."

"You are teasing me, Mister Lenin," I say, and we both smile.

"I am," he says. "I am. But I promise this is not a wasted journey. I would like you to take a gift to someone for me. One of your beauty products. Could you do that?"

This change of tone pleases me. "I would be glad to. Are they an incorrupt person, like myself?"

He is already settling his narrow body back into his sarcophagus. "She is certainly beautiful. Inside and out."

HE SENDS ME to my Italy, to Florence. On the way, I bump into Az, who is interfering with a painting on the wall, one of Guido Reni's blue Saint Sebastians, and he nearly falls off his stepladder when he notices me.

"I wasn't stealing it," he says. "It was wonky and annoying me."

He hops down and kisses me twice on each cheek.

"Mister Lenin made a purchase tonight," I say. "A gift for someone he knows."

"Well, terrific. Hey, this time next year, you'll have him signed up to the scheme and doing hen nights. Just don't get into any discussions with him, okay? You know he had, like, the entire Romanov family rounded up and–" He blows a raspberry, spraying the corridor with finger-guns.

He is flippant enough, but I am struck by the violence. "Who were the Romanov family?"

"Just some dead folks in a basement."

He straightens his tie. It's uncommonly damp in this stretch of Cryptspace, and we are both uncomfortable.

39

The scent of roses only just smothers the mildewy hum of the stones softening under the rain's acid content, and I think of Mister Lenin's comments on Padre Pio's gym sock. Is it incorrupt, I wonder? In a thousand years, if there is any dry land left, will pilgrims flock to marvel at the white cotton, crisp and fresh as the day the Padre took it out of the drier? Or whoever did the washing for him, at least. I imagine a lot of household tasks are difficult when one bears the open wounds of Christ. Perhaps Mister Lenin identifies with that sort of disability, what with having no internal organs. It must be quite the handicap when attempting to make friends.

"Perhaps he isn't as bad as everyone says," I venture. "He seems pleasant enough. Chilly, but so would I be in that granite freezer they've got him in. Besides, I'm headed for Florence now. More my kind of climate."

Az is messing with the painting again, tilting the nude Sebastian this way and that, never once managing to set him dead central. "Florence? Say, he's not sending you to the temple of Venus, is he?"

"Venus?"

"Some Roman you are! The Goddess of beauty."

He is halfway transformed into the Venus de Milo, stony and naked, before I can turn my face away. "I really don't like it when you do that. Please."

"Oh! Terribly remiss of me." He lifts one marble arm-stump to cover his breasts. "The Romans had you killed, didn't they? What a time to be alive, though. The Colloseum. Gladiators fighting beasts. Human torches. Magnificent mucky human hideousness."

I look to poor, pierced Sebastian for strength. "I didn't like any of that. Aurelia did. My sister. I would often accompany her to the games. She liked..." I pause, unsure why the fragile matter of my memories causes my toes to curl in my sandals as if away from hot sand. "She liked the blood."

"Well, that's girls for you, isn't it? Barbarous. I knew a girl once who liked me to— Well. It doesn't bear repeating. I say, though, hadn't the Empire converted to Christianity when you were around? Emperor Constantine had a dream about Jesus, or something, his road to Damascus moment. How'd you manage to get martyred in a Christian country, you silly sod?"

He puts his restored arm around me as we walk. It's nice. I don't get a lot of hugs.

"I wish I knew."

As I say it, another rainstorm must have started over Italy. The Cryptspace stream swells and gathers pace, and the smell of roses is overtaken briefly by the cool ghost of far-off storm winds. Standing too close to the edge, Az's leather brogues receive a soaking, and he pats me on the back.

"There, there, pretty thing. Maybe you're better off not knowing."

I STILL DON'T understand Az's comment about Venus as I enter Florence. Those gods were washed away long ago.

I emerge from Cryptspace into what looks like a basement, and by feeling my way in the dark I discover the stairs leading up into the main chamber. It doesn't seem to be a temple, and it definitely isn't a church, and I'm wondering why I've been sent to such a white building with so many shelves of jars. Ugly florescent signs mark the exits. In the jaundiced light, I put my face close to one of the jars. There is a cauliflower inside.

I find her lying in an unadorned glass case. There is a pearl necklace close to her throat and a single plait of dark hair lying long and loose over one shoulder. She is sleeping, laid out languidly, like my own pose at home in Dubrovnik, but naked, covered by a mottled red cloth that doesn't quite protect her modesty. I don't wish to startle her, and so I stand off to one side, looking at the jars of floating matter, and cough.

She blinks and raises one limp hand to cover a yawn.

"Are you a burglar?" she asks.

"Madam. I have a gift for you. From Mister Lenin."

"I don't know anyone of that name."

"It's Russian Red lipstick by MAC. Suits almost every skintone."

"Did you say a gift?" Her face rolls in my direction. She is a stunning beauty. Every soul in Christendom harbours the light of beauty, in my opinion, but she truly is an uncommon specimen of wonder. I go to her like a dog.

But then, as with Lenin, I find myself doing something terribly rude. I stop short. My hand, clutching her gift, goes to my mouth.

"You must have been martyred most terribly," I say before I can stop myself. "The least they could do is put it all back inside."

"I can't hear you through this glass," she says. "One second."

I am trying not to look, but the poor girl is eviscerated. What I had taken for a mottled red blanket was in fact her. Her organs. Displayed. I get a sudden rank mental image of Aurelia, down in the kitchens of our villa, showing the slaves how to divine the future in the guts of a goat. She wipes the sweat from her brow with relish, painting herself a fierce rusty red as she throws a look over her shoulder at me.

"I read your fortune," Aurelia grins. "You don't want to know it."

I have dropped the lipstick. It rolls along the floor and I stoop to catch it. I notice an information panel like my sign at home in the church.

Anatomical Venus, 1840s. Also known as The Slashed Beauty or The Dissected Grace.

Alongside it, there is a reproduction of a nineteenth century broadside advertisement, shouting in many different fonts:

'Know thyself! Signor Sarti's celebrated Anatomical Venus (together with numerous smaller models of special interest to ladies) showing the marvellous mechanism of the human body, that small tenement in which the Soul of Man resides. Admission one shilling.'

As I am reading, the woman has unlocked the case and is sitting up. Her yellow lungs are wings where her breasts should be. Her intestines coil like a rope of blue rubies around her waist, and she regards me with the cool eyes of a martyr. I cannot think of a single word to say.

"You mentioned a gift," she says.

Open-mouthed, I nod.

"I like gifts."

I am incapable of the task of moving. Whatever she is, I have never seen anything so wonderful as her. Not in two-thousand years. Not even the sad girl from the shelter with her voice like clever birds can compare to this bloodless vision of God's greatest creation.

"Oh," I breathe. "I am glad he sent me to you."

She stretches out her long golden arm and takes the lipstick from me. She tests it on the back of her hand. "What a perfect red. You must thank this Mister Whoever. Did he see me at one of my shows, perhaps? I toured all the greatest cities of Europe with Signor Sarti, in my day. And you, who are you? I haven't met you before. I know I'd remember. I don't get visitors. Not ones I can talk to."

"My name is Silvan, madam."

"Are you going to a party?"

"I... what?"

"Your clothes are very pretty. Are you a Roman tonight?"

She means, am I wearing a costume? When I dumbly shake my head, I remember pilgrims talking about the disgraceful stag party they'd seen wending about the streets of Dubrovnik the week Rome went under. Drunken lads in togas and snorkels.

Even The Vatican couldn't save itself in the end. The Pope decided to spend what was left in the substantial Papal coffers to construct a floating basilica above the site of the old one. A sort of holy life buoy. There was poetry in the situation, he said. The cleansing of the flood. Nowadays, when one wants to see the streets of Rome, one must board one of the chugging, glass-bottomed vaporettos taking tourists around in circles, all day and all night. The city authorities deigned to install a series of yellow lights in the submerged streets so all one has to do is look down to see the pavements trod by Nero and Agrippa and even me. At Easter, they do a special underwater Mass down in the quiet dark.

"You've got a nasty wound there, Silvan," Venus remarks cheerfully. "You've come to the right place."

"What sort of shrine is this?"

"If you believe the guidebook, it's *a temple of de mind.*" Hammy Italian, mimicking, I suppose, the Signor Sarti from the sign. She treats me to a wry grin. "Look, pass me that box, will you?"

I go to the shelf she indicates. Among ornate syringes and wicked, shining knives there are glass vials of murky fluid, and I am reminded of the blood of poor beheaded Saint Januarius, coagulated in its golden ampoule. Three times a year, the priests of Naples bring it out and watch as the powdery mess becomes wet, miraculous blood

45

once more after hundreds of years. The two occasions the blood failed to liquefy, plague struck the city, and then an earthquake. I wonder what these receptacles before me mean. Offerings, perhaps, to this eviscerated woman? It feels pagan to me. Familiar, yet wrong.

"To the left," she says. "The box with the white cross on it."

It's a stubby, equal sided cross, and when I take the box to her, I see it is full of bandages and individually wrapped antiseptic wipes. And then I notice I can see her heart, a red and blue palmful of muscle, and I quickly avert my eyes. Because if that isn't intimacy, what is?

"Don't be shy. I'm designed to show off literally almost everything. Look. Penny for my thoughts?"

With this, she puts her hands to her face and lifts it away from her skull, a section of which is neatly cut away to reveal the wrinkled beige brain beneath. Her eyes are gigantic white balls that mirror my shock.

"There now," she says, replacing her face. "Nothing left to fear. Come here and let me clean up that cut."

I am now more afraid of her than of Mister Lenin. I kneel at her glass case for her to reach my throat and marvel at the muddle of parts inside of her. Brown kidneys, like beans. Rivers and tributaries of blood. Do I look like that, inside? Do my visitors? Shelter Girl? Somehow, I hope not. I prefer to think of humans as pulsing with secret, golden light, not meaty parts liable to smell and ultimately melt away. Just imagining Shelter Girl opened up like this fills me with revulsion and shame. '*That small tenement in which the Soul of Man resides*'. What rot. This Anatomical Venus was created not to ignite wonder of the works of God, but to satisfy prurient curiosity, to break apart a woman as one would a timepiece, ruining it forever.

I should never have agreed to come.

"This is deep," she remarks, dabbing at the painless gash in my throat.

"Yes. It killed me."

She wipes diligently, but the blood will not come off.

"How long have you gone without washing this properly?"

"Two-thousand years, or thereabouts."

"For goodness' sakes. Hygiene, boy. Are you a museum piece? How well your people have preserved you. If you walk further down this corridor, you'll see a bog mummy from around your time. She looks like a raisin."

"People don't care for me. God does." I say so defiantly, but it isn't strictly true. I get a going-over with a handheld vacuum cleaner once a week. But I am no museum piece, lying there inertly distracting the curious. I am unnatural. I prove the laws of the Universe to be nothing but playthings to the Creator. I blow open the mind, liberating it with the experience of true wonder. I wish to tell her all this, but she lounges there with her ribbons of guts, placid and lovely and very naked. Somehow, for all her pearls and braided hair, to prettify her with lipstick is to insult her grandeur.

Disgust. And wonderment. I am mixed up.

I flee this profane temple. As I hurry to the exit sign, I hear the disappointment in her voice. "You can come back, you know. Any time you like."

Outside, I hear the birds of dawn.

2

"The bleeding continued till many things were seen and understood."

> – *Julian of Norwich, 'Revelations of Divine Love' 1373.*

JOHANN WAITS FOR me at the gate, chewing his nails.

"It's nearly sunrise. You could have been locked out."

"I must organise my appointments more rigorously."

"You look troubled, friend."

I hurry by, but he comes to me, my favourite monk, his hands emerging from his voluminous sleeves to touch my face.

"Is it Lenin?" he says. "Has he done something?"

I am not yet sure. Johann lets me retreat to my bower where I lay myself down in my customary swoon, the one I have kept up since Rome ruled the world and Christ was a man almost within living memory.

"If you could see your face, Silvan…"

Aurelia is having her hair braided. I sit on the floor behind her, watching the slim hands of the slave girls building that coil she likes atop her head, making her taller. I see her face in the mirror, dark eyes fixed on me, and I deferentially look down.

"You look like an idiot in love," she says.

But I do love you, I want to say. I have always loved

50

you. You have always been here. That's what love is, isn't it? Devotion without end.

"I hope I don't look like that," she says.

She sees me tilt my head.

"Because *I* am in love," she says. A proclamation. I could almost be mistaken into believing she means it to hurt me, but I know her mastery over men and she is of a marrying age. No, I don't acknowledge that pang. "He has wealth and influence. And his biceps are like ham hocks. A soldier."

Now she is mocking me. She permits the slaves to giggle.

"But you aren't to worry," she says. "No. You're coming with me."

I GO BACK because I must. I have ignored another note from Thérèse and an invitation from Valerius and Deodatus. I trade their warm company for the misery of Russia, and the guard with the black beard who will let me in like a tradesman to a great house.

Across Europe, it has rained for nine consecutive days. I have heard the laywomen in the church. The British Prime Minister has once again attempted the evacuation of children from the remaining low-lying settlements to the highlands of the Scottish and Welsh republics. A rumour has spread that there is no plan in place to reunite the children with their families, and so people are refusing en masse, bundling babies into attics and airing cupboards. Separatist groups war for control over suburbs. Looters. Martial law. I spend my days in prayer, though behind my eyes I see the absurdity of a dead boy in sandals holding back the flood. It is a new sensation; one that puts an ache in my bones. I think it is shame.

"There is a saying here," remarks a familiar voice, accompanied by the flowery odour of sanctity. "'*Pray to*

God, but row for shore'."

"Bernadette."

She is paddling in the freezing Cryptspace stream, her skirts hitched up to the knee. I had thought my mood would make me averse to company, but the sight of her fills my heart.

"Everyone has been trying to reach you by post," she says, splashing. "I thought I'd take a more direct approach. Don't be cross with Johann. He told me where to find you, but only because I snatched up his music machine and threatened to drop it in a puddle."

We smile. She hauls herself from the water and squeezes both my hands.

"Russia's rather grim, isn't it?" she says. "People are disappearing into the forests again. Towns are too dangerous. It's funny. They always seem to turn into wild animals again, don't they, at times like these?"

"There isn't anything we can do."

"I do beg your pardon?" She says it as if I were a novice giving her backchat, but then she registers the dullness in my voice. "It isn't our task to change matters, *mon petit*. We're present. We listen. What else is there?"

"I know."

"Could you say that again, a little more sullenly?"

I do my best to smile for her. "I have to go, Bernadette."

But she takes hold of my shoulders – first raising herself on her tiptoes – and I catch the loveliest whiff of roses from her smooth white flesh as she presses her lips to my cheek. This is what her visitors see in her: serenity, unblemished by the world and its ugliness. Bernadette most certainly doesn't have kidneys like beans and tangled vessels of sticky blood.

"Do not be downhearted. You died for something, Silvan. Think of all the people throughout human history who never had the chance to lay down their lives for what they believe. God set you aside because you have the strength for the burden. It is expected for you to stumble. But you must promise me – you will come to me before the load becomes unbearable. *Oui?*"

I nearly go to her. A preserved Russian revolutionary won't be going anywhere overnight, and she and I could flee together. Talk. Laugh. We could go outside. I haven't been outside for…

I freeze.

I must ask permission to go somewhere alone.

Do I? I hear it in Aurelia's voice, in those fol-de-rol tones she used for anything distasteful. *Mother's fat slave is pregnant* or *Those cannibal Christians are skulking around again.* Yes, I remember her saying that. She misunderstood The Last Supper, the sacrifice of blood and flesh. Like so many Romans, she thought we worshipped death.

"If it's death they want…" I hear her say. "Why not let them have it?"

Bernadette is gone.

When I gather my courage to approach Lenin's mausoleum, he is waiting for me, his body propped up like an ironing board against his sarcophagus. He commits himself to a thin smile this time, but his face is so stiff with embalming fluid, it looks more like the beginnings of a sneeze.

"The boy bishop returns. What trifles do you have for me today, in your suitcase?"

"I didn't bring it with me."

"You have seen the error of your ways and come to me for tuition?"

"One of the wheels is broken." I linger at the entrance. But when he bids me come, I do so.

"I had hoped you would visit tonight," he tells me. "I have had a bath. My carers say I am developing black patches on my face and hands. They dipped me in some green watery agent... I forget the name, but it is most toxic. Like your churchmen, they are keen to keep up the illusion of eternity."

I sigh. I haven't the patience for his criticisms, not with images of the lovely unholy Venus still troubling me. But there is something in the way he speaks to me, a leading tone, and I find myself responding to it, like a boy might follow his teacher.

"What will happen to you, Mister Lenin? Eventually?"

"To this?" He swipes a hand over his empty chest. "Why, plain old decay. I am no miracle, or perhaps only a miracle of modern chemistry. No, I will one day wither, as we all do. Though I am not so naïve as to believe there is not an intricate dummy in a storeroom somewhere, awaiting my retirement. 'Doesn't he look lifelike?' the public will say, when I am long since dust." He chuckles. "But come. Come and sit. I have been reading the literature you left me. Your catalogue, here. Your manifesto."

His green finger holds the catalogue open on a picture of Saint Rita of Cascia, the Guardian Saint of Desperate and Impossible Cases. Since her death in 1487, her incorrupt body has been seen to shift in its glass case, and on many occasions even her eyes have opened, causing a gigantic stir amongst the faithful. Here, the catalogue's designers have opted for a youthful illustration of Rita receiving the wounds of Christ on her forehead, wreathed in golden threads of holy light. It's marketing waffle. Would you buy blusher from a seventy-six year old nun, let alone a nun who's been seventy-six since the fifteenth century and probably died of necrosis? We aren't all lucky enough to be martyred in our twenties.

But Mister Lenin, I feel, has taken it rather too literally.

"Beauty highlights what we lack," he says, slapping Saint Rita with the backs of his fingers. "Beauty equals wealth. It equals status. It equals desire, and, by extension, love. A kind of currency. You who call yourselves saints – all you do is present an unattainable ideal of goodness. In my lifetime, I was aware of the usefulness of the Church. The leaders, I knew, were powerful allies. But my dream was of a society where one man could stand shoulder-to-shoulder with another. Tell me – what could a peasant woman with holes in her shoes possibly see in your church of opulent perfection but all the things beyond her reach?"

I think of Shelter Girl, how she came to me for hope. How coming to me was an act of consciousness. A ritual all of her own. She could have prayed for my intercession from her cot in the shelter, couldn't she? But she chose a journey. And though there may be little I can do to help her, that does not preclude me from caring. That helplessness does not stuff my ears.

Still, she has not come back.

I attempt to get up, but Lenin tugs on my tunic and I plop back down beside him.

"And the Bible?" He continues. "From Proverbs: *'Favour is deceitful, and beauty is vain'*."

I groan.

"Hm? And this? *'Women adorn themselves in modest*

56

apparel, with shamefacedness and sobriety; not with braided hair, or gold, or pearls, or costly array'."

"Mister Lenin —"

"You will listen. *'And it shall come to pass, that instead of sweet smell there shall be stink; and instead of well set hair baldness; and burning instead of beauty'.* Isaiah, I believe. Putting me in mind of my own black spots."

My hand goes to my brow. I should be sweating, but of course, I cannot. "Please don't challenge me to a scriptural duel, Mister Lenin."

"Aha. Then you acknowledge your hypocrisy? You see that your holy book forbids you to do the very thing you dedicate your long life to? Shallowness. Deceit. Material wealth."

"It's just that I haven't read the whole thing."

His face is a green oval of shock, and I shrug.

"I haven't read the Bible. Look, I lived long before the Gutenberg press. Don't look so surprised. Anyway, fighting each other with ancient quotes translated several times over is one of the biggest timewasters out there. Take it from someone with all the time in the Universe to spare. What I do all day is listen to the prayers and confessions of people in need. No, I don't get up and pat them on the head, and I certainly don't pay their heating bills, or persuade the insurance companies to cover their medical expenses. What I can do is offer a glimpse of somewhere better. Where all of this is just a bad dream. And if that doesn't meet with your approval, Mister Lenin, then I'm afraid you will have to find your comfort somewhere else. And I hope that you do. But I must do what I must."

A rumble of thunder over Moscow. I expect Lenin to make an arch remark about God agreeing with me, but he doesn't. It is mid-April, but no true spring. I think back to a world where spring was a time of birth and fruitfulness. Toil and reap, toil and reap. You can buy genetically-engineered asparagus any time of the year, now, limp, anaemic. I feel old. I feel...

What am I doing here?

Lenin is watching me think. A strange softness has come over his face. "I had a brother once. He was not unlike you."

"Was he a religious man?"

"A student of natural sciences. A gentle young man. He, too, believed he must do what he must." Lenin lays the catalogue on the lip of his sarcophagus and allows it to slither to the floor. "He was executed, aged twenty, for plotting to set a bomb to kill the Tsar."

"I had a sister. She would approve of killing a king, I'm sure." I pause, let my teeth bruise the flesh of my lip. "Mister Lenin, I am sorry for your loss."

"By his death, I knew my calling." He is on his feet now, chin up, and I know these are words he has said a thousand times, but before he can launch into a speech, something falters. "Don't you miss your sister? Wouldn't you like to see your family, after all this time?"

"It isn't something I think about."

"That is what your authorities want, of course. You not to think."

"It's better than having me ushered into a basement and shot."

He isn't expecting me to know about the Romanovs. He flinches; a reflexive flash of the teeth. He is quiet for a long time after this, and I fancy I can hear the pounding of the rain outside, up past all these metres of granite where the sky hangs as it always has, infinite and black.

The catalogue lies where it fell. *'Breathing new life into age-old faith!'*

"Have you ever witnessed mass starvation, Silvan?"

I sigh. "I have heard the recent news."

"I don't mean mild hunger. Not the inconvenience of a flooded supermarket. I mean bones protruding from rags. I mean looking down at a departed neighbour and thinking, well, waste is a sin, and meat is meat…"

"It can't be long now."

"No."

He respects me for saying so.

"Some brutality is necessary," he says. "Your God would agree."

He means martyrdom. Myself, his brother. It moves people.

My finger brushes the mouth of my wound and he allows me to walk away from him. I am at the lip of Cryptspace when I pause to look at him.

"Mister Lenin, I like you very much, and we agree on many points. But you must know, I will not keep coming here if all we do is torment one another."

It is a silly thing to say in front of so savage an orator – a soft, Christian thing – yet when he opens his pale mouth to speak to me, he does so with the frankness of an equal.

"Like most purely decorative things, Silvan, you are empty on the inside."

I WILL GO to Valerius. He will greet me with one of his bony embraces and I will tell him about the inside-out girl and make him laugh with my anatomical observations. Here was your liver. Here was your spleen. Valerius, something is happening to me. Valerius, I am frightened.

In Germany, I am met by a monk at the gate. He has the frowny look of Martin Luther about him, that Protestant suspicion of Papal excess, but he soon treats me to a warm handshake and I feel guilty. Mister Lenin has made me wary of people. I must do better.

"I am sorry, venerable Silvan, but you cannot come inside tonight. There is a television crew filming a special service for the recent cholera victims."

Venus' open body intrudes; all those fallible organs. "Cholera? In Germany?"

"And France, and what's left of Poland. People were careful to begin with, but when the lorries stopped coming with the bottled water..."

He spreads his hands as if this should be obvious. As

if whole nations drinking their own filth is just one of those things. But this is Cryptspace – the monk is dead, like me. We see things differently.

I can hear them up above, singing. Fighting thirst.

Down here, it smells like roses.

JOHANN IS DOZING with his headphones in his ears. I pass unnoticed into Dubrovnik. Under the altar, I settle down into my customary position, my limbs slipping into those velvet nooks they have known for hundreds of years while the glass muffles the chaos outside.

Day slinks guiltily under the door. There are no visitors all morning, so the laywomen run a Hoover over the carpet. One of them suggests opening a small café at the church door. Simple food for a small donation. Free to those in need. That would at least be doing something. Or socks, said another. A dry pair of socks is what a refugee wants the most, next to getting his home back, and we all know that's never going to happen.

I sneak a glance at my feet. I'm not wearing socks to donate. I cannot even aspire to those levels of usefulness.

Cholera. I hope Shelter Girl is alright.

"Ave, Silvan."

God help me, I almost jump.

At first, I think it is Az. It sounds like him, carefree and spry, but the footfall is too heavy, nearing my bower.

Through my eyelashes, I see him. He is down on his haunches beside me. I can see each individual hair on his arms. The dirt under his fingernails. The meat of his thighs. I think of Venus and the terrible clockwork of the anatomy. The power this man's body alone affords him.

No, this is not Az.

"Did you think we had forgotten you, Silvan?" he says.

I cannot forget that severed thumb. He rests it on his thigh, a glistening red jewel.

"Decimus."

The name forces its way out from whatever deep chamber I have kept it, all these centuries. It sets the nerves at the base of my spine singing, a knife of a noise that attacks my ears and makes me dizzy. He knows this, of course. There is nothing he does not know.

He smiles and my whole body jolts.

I must have dozed off.

I dare to open my eyes and look about the room for him, but I am alone with the winking green light of the fire exit. Outside, a government lorry chugs by, blasting information on a loud speaker. *Identity cards must be carried at all times. Water-sanitising tablets still available. The black market is the enemy of recovery.* Yes, I must have been dreaming.

But I don't sleep. I haven't since I died. We don't.

Decimus is gone. The wet sandal prints on the tiles are not.

I pray for night.

NIGHT DOES NOT come. Shelter Girl does.

She is a shipwreck in borrowed clothes, her knotty wrists protruding from the frayed sleeves of her Disney sweater. She has lost flesh. The smells of the shelter are all around her, and she is ashamed, but when she bows before the altar and kneels beside me, she is smiling.

"Hello, Silvan."

Hello, friend. I've been thinking of you.

"My husband is better," she says. "He's eating more normally, anyway. I've been giving him my rations. I faked a stomach bug, but they take diarrhoea really seriously and they've put me on this electrolyte water that gives me palpitations."

She checks we are not being watched and settles down with her legs out beside her, one arm braced to take her meagre weight as she dips her head so close to mine that her breath mists the glass.

"I'm sorry I was so negative last time. Here, look. Good times. Last autumn's harvest festival."

She holds up the photograph. I see a happy band of

urchins crammed together under a tarpaulin. Bales of wheat. Wheels of white cheese. A brace of pheasants are held up by an old man with the longest dreadlocks I've ever seen. Shelter Girl stands centre, laughing, holding up a jar of golden honey so heavy her biceps are bulging. A painted banner held by many hands reads, '*If the bees die, we die*'. A child has added drippy yellow bumblebees. That's him, I think, noticing a grubby little person hugging Shelter Girl's baggy jeans. Few look at the camera. The eyes, the smiles – all are for her.

They loved her, these people. She was a leader.

"I had a dream about you," she says. "You were outside, sleeping on the ground, only the ground was dry and dusty. You were on your back, like you are now. It was night, and there were people peeking out of alleyways to look at you. As if they were hungry. As if you might be food." She shifts, her jeans mopping up the water from Decimus' sandals. "I think it was a holy dream. But what does it mean?"

I AM KNEELING to dust the household gods. The Lar, dancing spirit of hearth and home, has been given an offering of honey cake. The Goddess Venus has been offered honeycomb; naked and washing her hair, she ignores it. Aurelia likes to bring the figurines out for feasts. Venus gets to stand amongst the meat, a beauty bathing in the juices. My sister's unique artistic sensibilities have won her a fine husband who lays on parties for his legion friends and their wives. She wears bracelets of braided gold, and he, fresh from the senatorial provinces of Macedonia, carries his vitis staff with him, even to dinner. A vitis staff of laurel wood. His men call him Fetch Me Another; he is always breaking it over their backs.

"Decimus says there was a time we didn't worship Venus. He says we stole her from the Macedonians."

Aurelia is eating grapes, poised behind me. She spits the pips onto the tiles. She can do anything she likes. Mother isn't here to remonstrate.

"While he was in Macedonia, Decimus says he saw

66

Christians, too. They weren't like the ones here. They wore hair shirts and whipped themselves with branches. I hope the Emperor doesn't decide to steal *that*, too."

A grape bounces off my head.

"Are you not speaking to me?" She comes to me and pulls back the neck of my tunic where my long hair covers the skin. She usually makes some comment about how embarrassing it is to be seen with a man who wears his hair like a girl, though I know she loves the unusual colour of it, and its softness. This time she swipes it aside. Her voice drops to a blue murmur and I feel her pull the tunic down to the stubs of my shoulderblades.

"How did you get these marks?" she asks.

She needn't ask. I am his slave now, as much as hers.

I RISE FROM my bower as soon as the laywomen have snuffed the church candles and locked the door. There were no more visitors after Shelter Girl and the church lacks that holy aroma I know better than that of my own body, ever faithful beneath the whiff of candles and the polished oak. Humans. Rows of living human bodies. This place smells like a vacant tomb.

I must say it out loud. I must speak the word before I lay eyes on another soul.

"Slave."

I remember no family before Aurelia. I recollect no slave ship, no manacles, nor the long climb onto the auction block. There is only her, the little girl I remember now – I *know* now – I was bought for. A purchased playmate. I suppose they chose me for my looks. Why spend money on anything plain?

I raise a hand to my face. My nose is delicate, like a Persian girl's. My cheekbones Slavic. These are the sole clues to my birth, and I long ago abandoned probing them for answers. I made that decision. I must have.

What other decision is a slave permitted to make?

Slave.

I turn my back to the altar and go down to Cryptspace. Johann is waiting, little Johann who died of smallpox. His chastity and poverty didn't immunise him one jot. He is listening to his music. The earbuds leak sound; I hear an odd warbling drone and touch his sleeve. He smiles and offers the earbuds to me.

"The Music of the Spheres," he says. "The planets emit electromagnetic waves that translate to music. Space symphonies. NASA recorded the songs of every planet in this solar system. This is Venus. Listen."

He cups my face to insert the alien device into each ear. I hear hazy voices ringing in the vastness. Distant echoes of words I do not know. Deep. Woeful. Like the private thoughts of God.

It is not pretty. Not in the least.

I lie on the Cryptspace stones and listen for a full hour.

I HAVE APPOINTMENTS, but I don't make them. I sit among my cosmetics. Tubes roll on the marble around me, paints of pink, fuchsia, puce, mauve, and frailest lily white. Aurelia's slave girls – her *ornatrices*; God, I am remembering the words – began their mornings caressing her face with creams of chalk and orris root. They sculpted the bones of her cheeks with rouge and made a canvas of the creases of her eyelids; shadows of saffron and a fearsome rim of kohl. Decimus would often intrude upon this ritual, interrupting the slaves' delicate work to kiss his wife, to drag his teeth down the white column of her neck and make promises that caused me to blush, sitting as I always did, at the back of the room, ready to fetch her whatsoever she desired. I was the first man in her life, if a slave could be termed a man, and my presence during these feminine sacraments bothered him not a little. I see him now, the thick, tanned trunk of him turning to look upon me.

"We should make him watch."

No, I will not access those mornings, nor those nights.

Rome is sunk and I am blessedly alone, here with my paints in my church without a congregation.

At least, I assumed I was alone. Az is here, licking an ice cream cone and peering over my shoulder.

"Mind you don't spill that Dior lip tint. It's more expensive than gold." He waggles the ice cream under my nose. It's vanilla with ribbons of strawberry sauce and beginning to melt. "Johann said you needed perking up. This was the most legal stimulant I could bring you at such short notice."

I take the thing and give it a tentative open-mouthed kiss. I haven't attempted food for eons, and when a sad trickle of ice cream flows from the wound in my throat and down my tunic I remember why.

"See," he sighs. "I was going to bring you something snortable, but I thought you'd get upset. Give it here. Waste not."

He polishes it off in seconds while I sit in silence.

"Did you know I was a slave?" I ask quietly.

He brushes the crumbs of cone from his hands, wiping them on his jolly picnic blazer. "Who told you that?"

"I remembered."

Az gives a long sigh that puffs out his cheeks. "Wow," he says. "What can I say? Condolences?"

I feel emptied out, like Mister Lenin. Exposed, like Venus.

Az sits beside me, on the floor. His face is so young, the skin soft and full. It is absurd to me. A fallen angel, a rebel against God, who is, by anyone's estimation, cute.

"I've met slaves before," he says. "You'd think they'd be angry, and a lot of them are. But most just sort of… drift. A bit like grief, I suppose." There is a crust of dried mud on the turn-ups of his trousers, and he flicks it off with a fingernail. "Of course, I've met slave owners, too. They're a contented bunch, right up until they die. Then they're all products of their time, willing to learn, happy to change. All terribly reasonable folks."

I will not speak to him of Decimus. I realise now Az's transformation into his physical form that first night in front of my altar was him sensing that shadow in my mind. He drew it out. I should, I suppose, be grateful for his help.

He claps me on the knee. "But hey, you're a success story. You're the little bishop who could. You broke out of an antiquated, unfair system, struck out on your own, and made something of yourself. A bit like I did."

I blink back surprise. "You fell from heaven."

"But the fall," he says, "was a teacher."

A CONTAGION FLOODS Imperial Rome. Twenty-four hours after complaining of a sore throat, you're dead in your own lavatory. Fourteen of Decimus' men die this way, together in the communal facilities at the barracks, soiled drawers bunched around their ankles. Hardly a soldier's death, Decimus says, touching his vitis staff. When he thinks I notice the fear behind his jollity, he crosshatches my legs with welts.

Our household goes untouched by the fingers of death. When one of the slaves coughs while bringing out the dinner wine, Decimus calmly stands, takes the man by the neck and throws him out, tumbling down the stairs of the villa. No one wants his few possessions, so we burn them. I keep the household gods appeased with gifts of honey and perfume. Aurelia says I must be pleasing them, so healthy we all are. Perhaps it is my face.

Mother dies. She doesn't go the way of the plague victims; far too common. Being dressed, she remarks she can no longer feel her left arm. By evening, she is dead.

For her funeral in the outskirts of the city, we have to travel past the mass plebeian graves, white with quicklime. They can't bury the bodies fast enough; the dead are lined up toe to toe in their hasty shrouds. Aurelia covers her mouth. A knot of men, unfashionably bearded yet decently dressed, loiter a short distance from the pit, talking and gesticulating amongst themselves at the gates separating the living city and the open land of the revered dead.

"Christians," Aurelia tells me. "They're probably enjoying this."

They sense her glare. As the funeral party passes by, the men bow their heads in deference to the bereaved, but this is not acceptable to Decimus. He breaks away from his wife to wave at them, good cheer plastered all over his handsome face even as the flies settle on his skin.

"Gentlemen. How is your friend, the bishop Romanus?"

The leader of them, a big man with a red beard, shouts back: "The governor burned his church. In prison, they cut out his tongue."

"Did they indeed? I thought he would never run out of things to say."

"You are a wicked man," says another. "Emperor Constantine will not allow this to continue."

The three others nod at the judgment. To me, they look powerful and grave, but my master treats them like players in a comedy. Decimus leaves the road and strolls to them, that slow swagger I know to fear, his vitis staff tucked under his arm like a promise.

"Indeed? Romanus disrupted the traditional sacrifices. Whatever intellectual pretensions our beloved Emperor harbours, he is not so lofty as to deny his people the worship of the true gods. All his most trusted men spit on your Christianity. I, for instance. My soldiers. The sons my wife will bear me…"

"May God strike her barren."

There is a dreadful moment in which Red Beard looks as if he cannot believe what has just escaped his mouth. Cheeks flushed, my master visibly fights the yearning to run him through. All the household slaves hear the curse and hold our breaths. We are a superstitious lot.

Circling gulls intrude upon the hush.

"I would cut out every Christian tongue in the empire, if I could," Decimus tells the Christians, conversationally. "I would have my wife's slaves sew them into garlands and hang them in every room of our house. I would roll them up and stuff them with rice and feed them to my honoured guests along with dormice and salted fish. Festivity, gentlemen! I would invite you to my table, but I hear your god forbids pleasure of any kind."

Beside me, on the road, Aurelia rolls her eyes. "Husband, come."

He doesn't hear her. The procession has stopped. Aurelia slaps my arm.

"Go and get him, Silvan."

"My lady?" I am dragging the sacrificial sow and the other slaves look blankly at me as I raise the leash, hoping for someone to take over.

In the end, Aurelia snatches it from me. "Go."

I go to the lip of the grave, covering my mouth against the terrible grasping reek. The sight of the pit – the depth, the sheer lumpen *fullness* of it – lances me with nauseous terror and I forget my mistress' orders. My mouth is dry with revulsion, yet still I peer inside at the shapes of men and women and children, steaming in the swampy sun as the assembled workers prepare to throw in another layer of dead. Decimus is busy toying with the Christians and does not see me until he notices their attention wavering. They are looking past him at me, all of them, four sets of eyes taking me in with what? Surprise? Fascination? I am used to stares, but what would a death worshipping Christian find so interesting in a slave? I bow my head, as much to escape their searching looks as to appease Decimus, who is glaring at me, coming to spoil his fun.

"Forgive me, sir," I say, as softly as I may. "My lady is keen to continue on.

This, the Christians enjoy; the chiding of the great centurion Decimus by his little lady wife. The leader smiles through his red beard. "Your young slave is more courteous than you, Decimus. You have much to learn from him."

I think he knows the moment it leaves his lips that he has damned me.

Decimus inclines his head to look at me. The Christian's hand rises, palm out, tremulous, as if he can stop what he knows he has put into motion.

"Forgive you?" Decimus says.

He shoves me. The pit sweeps up to collect my falling body and I land on a pile of soft-hard corpses. They sink to accommodate me, rolling towards my weight. There are sounds. Gurgles. Wheezes. I know to keep my eyes tightly closed. The quicklime will blind me. I will be a blind slave, no good to anyone. I will be cast out, I will sleep in the open, I will beg under the arches with the old women and their foul chickpea soup and my body will fail me and one day I will be thrown into a pit with others on top of me, layer after layer, blocking out the sun. Panic so intense I think I will die of it. I choke on foetid air, my arms waving about in front of me like a man impaled, clutching at merciless nothingness, mewling like an infant, lips pressed together, for each time they burst open to scream I taste death and it lasts for eternity.

Living hands grab my wrists. Living men grunt, heaving me up. My sandalled feet sweep across the faces of the dead, my toenails catch on lips and eyelids, and I sob as they lay me on the ground.

I will never open my eyes. I lay curled in on myself. Aurelia and Decimus have gone with the rest of the funeral party, my rescuers tell me. They are Christians. They will take care of me.

All will be well.

MY BODY IS all there is of me that night. My spirit is elsewhere, hiding. They promise to bathe my body. They say they will feed it and give it clean clothes. They want nothing in return and they will send it back to my master with gifts to calm his ire.

I brace myself for a temple, one unlike any other I have seen in my life. Death worshippers, Aurelia had said. Instead, they take me to an ordinary house – a rather lowly house compared to that of my owners – with simple tiled floors and a leak in the kitchen roof. They take away my soiled clothes and bring water. I see a wooden cross on the wall and remember these are strange people with unwholesome beliefs and to be seen with them is to invite the worst kind of gossip. The four of them still stare at me. Only Red Beard dares to touch me, dipping a cloth in the scented water and lifting it to my face.

They fear the pestilence. But their looks are inquisitive.

"Did my master burn your temple?" I ask.

"And many others," he says.

I fear he will take revenge on me, his enemy's property. But there is kindness in his eyes, and regret. When he resists the urge to squeeze my bruises or pour vinegar on the old welts put there by my master, I feel a conspicuous lack of the dread I live with inside Decimus' walls. There was a time when I felt safe almost constantly – in Mother's cool, quiet house. I curse myself. I missed the final chance to say goodbye.

"I'm sorry," I whisper, and I mean it.

Red Beard squeezes out the cloth. "You are an innocent."

"I am a slave."

He ponders this. As the others dress me in a clean tunic and belt, and brush the tangles from my hair, Red Beard does something odd. Taking my face in both his hands, he stands tall before me, smelling of sweat and sandalwood. "There is neither Jew nor Aramaean," he tells me, "neither servant nor free person, neither male nor female, for all of you are one in Yeshua The Messiah."

I leave as soon as I can. They give me gifts of wine for Decimus, but I cannot take them. He will accuse me of stealing. I have already missed Mother's funeral, and such a thing is punishable most severely. Red Beard watches me leave, standing in the doorway with a lamp and whatever other riddles his religion has left to worry me with.

But I have faith only in my master's vitis staff.

I TELL ALL this to Thérèse of Lisieux. I go to her basilica in France hoping for a stiff dose of good sense, or at least the reassurance that I am too stupid and shallow for this sort of soul-searching and should be rescued immediately. Perhaps she can arrange for my glass bower to be glued shut with me in it.

"That," I tell her, "must have been how it began. I met the Christians. They taught me. I ran away to Greece and became a martyr."

We sit on simple chapel chairs, not looking at one another.

"It must have been so, in those early days of the Church," she says quietly, her face wreathed in roses. "Strange meetings. Changed lives."

"It's like living it all afresh. I was a slave, Thérèse. I remember the beatings. I remember the tedium. How am I to reconcile what I am now with the ugliness of what I was then?"

She lifts her perfect waxen hand to the wound at my neck.

"Brutality is romanticised in our faith. Our deaths made lovely, like heroes in ancient sagas. But life is an ugly business. You never had much of a story. You are too old for records to verify; you have been passed from nation to nation. Your loveliness in death is all you can truly offer, but what a gift that is. You are incorrupt, Silvan. God has singled you out for something astonishing – to be the impossible. All the rest... it doesn't matter."

I think of that pit of white lime and the shrouded figures piled within. In all my centuries of lovely death, it never occurred to me what should naturally have happened to my flesh. And what of my soul? If beauty is all I ever had to offer, what then if one day that magic is taken from me? I cannot look at my own hands, golden and hairless, untouched by toil.

"I hear the laywomen talking of atrocities," I say. "There are more slaves in the world today than at any other time in human history. I could use my experience to bring strength to those in need. There's a woman from one of the shelters. She was once a leader of lost people. I could help her. Mister Lenin believes in a classless society. I could go to him. I could learn from him."

"Silvan, no."

"He is an intellectual. Not like me."

"I said no."

"I ask to be used. I don't understand."

"Neither do I. Silvan, what if this is not the work of God? Have you considered the alternative? Who runs this company you work for? Why, after two-thousand years and more, would such a thing sprout up? Beauty products for blessed martyrs... who would dream up such a thing?"

I cannot tell her about Az. He is a creature trying to better himself, and she'll only judge him on his past. I have done good. Ask Shelter Girl. In fact, I will go home this instant and work magic on my face with pearl bronzer and a contour brush so her heart will swell with delight when she sees me next. I tug my tunic down as I stand and make for the door like a sulking boy, my hair hanging lank over my eyes and a tremor in my lip.

Thérèse watches me go with dismay. "Silvan, you must be cautious. What if someone is playing a trick?"

SOMEONE HAS LEFT a clownfish beside my bower during the night.

I take it for dead, lying still in a small puddle of seawater, but when I curl my hands around it, the little fish stirs as if from sleep and *kicks* with its tail.

"You want some water for that?"

It's Az, lounging in the front row, a martini glass in his hand.

"Is that water?" I ask him.

"Close enough." He saunters up, curious for a peek at the struggling fish. "Ah, a little Amphiprion. These chaps are interesting, actually. Clownfish live among sea anemones. A mutually-beneficial arrangement. Staying close to the anemone assures the survival of the fish, and the fish's leftover food sustains the anemone. Of course, in the early years of climate change, anemones began to lose their distinctive colouring. No more purple. No more green. Poor fish didn't know what home looked like anymore."

He holds out the glass, and I ease the fish into it. At

first it doesn't realise what the familiar embrace of water means, until the gills ripple gently and life returns in full.

Az smiles. He cups my cheek and kisses me on the lips.

"THEY WILL SAY how careless marriage has made me. First, Aurelia loses her mother, now her favourite slave."

My master and mistress lounge on the terrace with wine. From my hiding place in the garden I can see Aurelia's kohl is smudged. At her side, on his couch, Decimus runs a finger up her ankle.

"I will a send a slave-catcher after him. Where would he go, anyway? He has no talents, no trade. He will come back the moment he gets hungry." He takes her hand and presses his lips to her moonstone ring. "And then I will break his legs."

"Decimus. That is frowned upon."

He teases out a smile. "Not by anyone who matters. My father knew how to treat a slave. By the gods, he did. Not a single one ran away from our household – too frightened. A tool with legs, that's a slave. Your problem is you're too like your mother. Gods grant her peace. She had every opportunity to mould that boy into a regular marvel, but instead she convinced him he was a lapdog. If it were up to me, I'd breed him with one of the others

– that Germanic girl from the kitchens, Whatshername – and make pretty children to sell at a profit. I may still do it, if he comes back. Give him something to occupy himself with."

Aurelia morosely accepts a dish of olives from the Egyptian serving girl. "I hope he comes back."

"He will. He loves you. Almost as much as I love you."

"Is that why you dislike him?"

"Who said I dislike him? I tolerate him. It is no different from possessing a comely statue or an exotic plant. Only this particular weed would plant his seed in my wife."

She is laughing now, and he is motioning for the slave to pour more wine. It is my moment to appear quietly in the doorway, head bent, hands open.

Decimus sees me first, with those keen army eyes. "Ah! It returns."

"I came upon a fig tree, sir. Madam." I have brought them fruit. In the end, I hadn't the courage to return without platitudes.

Aurelia is struggling to hide her relief, but like Mother when Aurelia stayed out too late, she delivers her punishment from behind cold barricades. "Well, I don't want a fig. Do you, husband? No. We don't want your silly figs. You were embarrassing today. Of all days. Don't come near me for another week. I have cut your wine allowance. And your meat. You're spoiled. I am the mistress here."

It is only the latest in a million such outbursts, but it is better than a blow, so I take my fruit and go. My clean clothes feel traitorous against my skin. I can feel the coarse hands of the Christians still; their gentle ministrations. In the privacy of my room – I do not sleep with the other slaves and never have, a little privilege from my mistress that makes me unpopular – I remove the unfamiliar tunic and sit on my bed with my head in my hands. The day's horrific images flood towards me and I crush my lip between my teeth to frighten them away.

"You made my wife cry."

The voice of my master makes me jolt. He lounges massively in my doorway. There is a glass of wine in his hand and a quirk of amusement on his lips. I knew I'd got off lightly.

"She buried her mother today," he says, coming down into my little room. "She stood there like marble and bore it all with dignity. But you made her cry."

She was my mother too, I think with surprising vehemence. He settles down beside me on the bed. The width of his thighs has always astonished me, like those of a warhorse. He wears the scars of battle like golden chains, thick and proud; nothing like the lacy work he makes of my back. I expect him to add to his canvas tonight, but while I wait, eyes down, for him to make his first blow, Decimus is watching me. He has never paid me much attention. He reserves his energy for the buxom girls in the kitchen and Aurelia's pretty ornatrices, though none of them have yet fallen pregnant. I am his wife's amusement and nothing more. As a fighting man and a leader of others, he sees my uselessness and despises it. But his fingers are chillingly gentle as he takes my chin and tilts it this way and that, examining with wordless interest the shape of my jaw and the quality of my teeth.

Ah. He means to use me like a kitchen girl. It is testament to my stupidity that it has not occurred to me before.

"You have no idea where you come from, do you?" he says.

"Sir?"

"Have you even the wit to ask?"

He awaits my answer, draining his wine. I will say something incorrect and he will strike me for it. I am too frightened to speak, half-naked beside him, and he sighs.

"Aurelia's mother bought you from the block." His eyes are big, like a man talking to a child. "Yes? But before that?"

"I don't know, sir."

He snorts; I feel the heat of his breath against my face. "With Britons, it's laziness. With Germans, it's the smell. But you coastal yokels have fish for brains, I do declare it. Not so much as a whisper of curiosity."

"Coastal? Sir?"

"Think, boy. Can you think? Can you recall a memory, like a man?"

I remember feet. They rush to me – dusty white feet. Small toes gripping hot stone. I realise where I have seen such things before. Chalk is applied to the feet of slaves newly imported from foreign lands. The feet, I realise, are my own. My eyes flick up to meet my master's.

"Illyricum," he says. "I asked the old woman not long ago, and a good thing, too, considering. Illyricum, in the East, over the Sea of Adria. You're a little tribal brat, Silvan."

He pats me on the back. I stare about me in confusion. Illyricum. I have never thought of myself as anything less than Roman. As anything other than Aurelia's. I knew well enough that I must have come from somewhere, but it had not mattered to Mother, and so it had not mattered to me. Decimus drops this information on me like a collar of iron. Illyricum. Yellow rock and salty air. And I?

"Yes, Illyricum…" Decimus goes on. "I said to my wife, my money was on Macedonia. The slave ships – unofficially, mind you – raid a good few coastal towns in that area to make up the numbers."

In Macedonia, they worship dirty drunkard gods and divine the future by breathing noxious fumes from the burning earth. Again, the white toes grip the stone, and my head reels with the thought of where I might be now, had Mother not handed over coin for me that day. Worse still, further back, the moment my fate toppled over, when an entrepreneurial Roman noticed me playing amongst the trees and said, "Good gods. That one. His *face*." No, I am no Macedonian, no more than I am a Christian, or a fig tree. In my mind, I flee to Illyricum, hunker down inside those coastal fortifications, deep in the yellow rock cloaked by the warm sea where Decimus cannot find me.

"You know what they say, of course," he tells me. "'*It is beautiful to die before becoming a slave*'. Fortune has abandoned you. But I am a thoughtful man. I don't despise you. Before long, it will be Saturnalia, and I have a gift to give you."

The giving of gifts is strictly between equals. Even at Saturnalia, that time of great revelry and the overthrowing of the natural hierarchy, a gift from one's master can hide a sting. I have heard of a slave who dropped a crystal goblet given to him in jest by his mistress – the boy was drunk, as was everyone – and she had him thrown to the lampreys. Decimus is less imaginative in his punishments. Or so I hope.

"I plan a magnificent party this year. I've paid for dancers, and fine costumes, and rivers of wine. A fortune teller will spin stories. And of course, food. Mountains of it. I have imported spices to make the eyes water with pleasure."

"Thank you, sir." I stare at the floor. "Most generous."

"You will not be there."

I search his face. My open fear makes him laugh.

"You are going to run away," he says.

I begin to deny it. I would never abandon my household. I would sooner die than leave my sister. Decimus holds up a finger.

"Run. Run away. You have my word I will send no man to search for you. I will send you off with a little money, a little food. And you will go far from here. Perhaps you will go and live with your Christian friends and their dead god. There are plenty of them in Macedonia. But you have my permission. Run."

"Sir, my mistress—"

"Aurelia will be grieved for five minutes. But then I will buy her a monkey, and a sleek white horse, and a dress spun from the threads of the Eastern provinces. And she will forget you."

There are tears in my eyes. In the ritual of manumission – the freeing of slaves – the master is permitted one final hard slap, signifying the end of the slave's subjugation. I feel I have been slapped. I do not feel free.

"She is my sister," I whisper brokenly.

He tweaks my nose so hard I fear it will snap. "If you say that again, I will beat you, for it is a lie, and I am not a man to tolerate lying. Run. It is the best day for it. I hurt you, did I not? Cruel Decimus. Fetch Me Another, my men call me, do they not? Poor little slave. Poor little lapdog."

"What if I want to stay?"

Decimus smirks. "You don't want that."

He takes a fig, bites down. Purple flesh, juicy as a bruise.

THE FOLLOWING NIGHT, I am convinced. Decimus has worked me hollow. The responsibilities of the serving girls, the Egyptian messenger boys, and even the gardeners are piled onto my back until I am sore in body and heart. Aurelia doesn't bother to smile at my discomfort. I have truly hurt her by making a scene at Mother's funeral, and my every attempt to please her is met with a glacial expression of boredom.

"I think my next pet will be a girl. What do you think, my love? A lovely blonde Gaul. Perhaps a gymnast, to entertain the guests?"

"All things can be arranged," my master says, looking past me at the garden, the long stretch of land leading down into the town and away to the docks leading East.

I take my figs. Decimus has left money and a cloak and the name of a man who will transport me. It is Illyricum I am dreaming of as I slip away, not my sister's grief at the loss of me, brief as it will be. I have not slept since my fall into the pit, and perhaps it is the lingering terror that has turned my brain. Night gives me courage.

City slaves are a dissolute lot, given the chance, and there are many of us on the streets this evening, heading for the brothels and the taverns. The occasional taste of pleasure drains the fervour from our rebellious dreams, I have often heard it said. To think, I never had any.

I swallow the lump in my throat. A man will be waiting for me at the river. A ship bound for Illyricum. I can smell the water.

"Silvan. You are unharmed?"

Guilty, I spin around. It is the red-bearded Christian. He has a jar of wine.

"I feared he would brand your face," he says.

I find my voice. "It's in the past."

"Already? You could go to the courts, Silvan. Excessive cruelty is no longer tolerated, even towards slaves."

And put Aurelia through such a public ordeal? I wouldn't consider it. And what constitutes excessive in an Empire where Decimus can hire contractors to come and crucify me in the garden if he so desires? They'll even mop up afterwards.

"Would you like a fig?" I asked him. "I have nothing else to repay your kindness."

He stares at the fruit in my outstretched hand. I don't know why he insists on wearing that astonished expression. You'd think I were a talking horse, the way he carries on.

"What you said as I left your home…" I said. "About there being no servants and no free men in your religion. Do Christians not keep slaves?"

Red Beard tears his gaze away from the fig. "Of course we do. Imagine if everyone freed their slaves tomorrow. The poor would suffer terribly. No work for the free-born, no, not when there are thousands of ex-slaves willing to do it for half the price. You see the uproar during Saturnalia, when the slaves may do as they please. No, that quotation is meant only to suggest that for God the Father a slave is still as capable of goodness as a free-born man."

Oh. I feel an unexpected disappointment. I can hear the boats on the river, the calls of the sailors coming into port for an evening's fun. Illyricum. The yellow hills.

Red Beard regards me with concern. "Silvan, you haven't run away, have you?"

I tell him my master's plan. In the chaos of Saturnalia, a slave may slip away, particularly when he is as unimportant as I. Red Beard takes my arm and pulls me into a secluded alcove, and I almost collide with a stranger slipping out of the shadows, a smiling youth in outlandish striped garments. A woman, perhaps, I correct myself, but then she is gone. I am exhausted. Seeing phantoms.

"Don't be a fool," the Christian tells me. "Even if Decimus permits you to leave, he has not freed you. If he changes his mind, or if one of his men recognises you, you face severe punishment. Perhaps death. And if you do succeed? An escaped slave is still a slave, in the eyes of your gods, and mine. All you will accomplish is distance. Ask yourself, why did he not legally free you? This could be sport to him. A hunt. After what he did to you in public—"

I shake my head. He wouldn't understand. I barely do. And he is making that face again, staring so intently at my eyes, my mouth, my hair… People stare at my master and mistress, but only because they are wealthy and elegant and both beautiful as gods treading the earth. I am a slave, I tell myself. As a child, as a man, and ever after.

"I have never met anyone like you," the Christian says quietly. I stand as still as I may as he puts down his jar of wine and reaches for me. He touches me, the firm pads of his thumbs tracing my cheekbones and the sockets of my eyes. "I worried Decimus would brand your face. Christians believe God created us in his own image. The human face… the wonder of it… is the closest we have to looking into His eyes, in this life."

He exhales lengthily, holding me still. In the dark streets, the passers-by seem not to see us, frozen here, face to face. He is about to say something more. His eyes hold a question. But a cry goes out somewhere behind him and we spring apart like conspirators as a woman, swathed in a long cloak, strides at us, fists balled.

"What is the meaning of this?" It is my sister. My stomach lurches as I envision lampreys and whips and broken bones.

The Christian puts himself between me and her. "I commandeered your slave, Madam. Forgive me. I noticed him at the evening markets and took him home to give him this wine for you and your husband."

"I don't want wine. I want him."

Her cheeks are red. At first, I think she has been running, but my mistress would surely never lower herself so. She seizes me by the back of my cloak and tugs me away like an errant child, leaving the Christian standing in the dark. I will not see him again.

"Saturnalia soon," she says under her breath. "The world will turn upside down, and then be put back to rights."

I see the fingernail furrows on her face and say nothing.

GERMANY. A POLICE cordon flutters in the draught where I emerge from Cryptspace eager for the sage company of Valerius. In the darkness, I mistake him for Deodatus at first. I didn't know his head was detachable. Nearing his golden bower, I am struck by the horrible absence of his jewels.

Desecration.

I kneel before him, dull with shock. "Who did this to you?"

He regards his toes, folded next to his jaw. In taking his jewels, the thieves cut the wires holding his bones together. My friend is in pieces and my old heart hurts.

"Oh," Valerius remarks mildly. "Some frightened men. Pays their passage to Africa, you see. Dry land. My heavy metal children were blamed. Most unjust."

"Defilement," I whisper. Why, when Man feels small, does it always come down to this? Smash and grab and run. "I will find replacements. I will ask Az. Would you mind them being paste, for the time being? I can't bear—"

"Ask who?"

"Az. My friend. He brings me cosmetics."

His glittering eyes are gone, but I know he is staring at me. "Silvan. You should have come to me. You should have confided in someone."

"Why?"

There is a shout from above. Water comes splattering down onto the flagstones and a hunk of ceiling masonry takes out the gilded lectern. In the dark, I can make out Az's picnic blazer and his smile peeking through the hole in the roof. "I say!" he calls down. "Did you know the little toerags also took the lead tiles? It's almost dawn, Silvan. You'd best get back to Croatia."

I can't bear the sight of Valerius a moment longer. I do as I am told.

IF THIS IS the end of the world, will you tell us?

My clownfish circles in his martini glass. Better cared for than most humans in the remaining world, I feed him and talk to him and offer all the reassurance I have to give. It is not the first time, of course. Whoever left me this fish knows that.

Aurelia's dress is red. She is carrying a glass bowl. "Don't look at me like that," she says, coming down the steps into my room. "I am your mistress, and it's nearly Saturnalia. No one will mind me giving you a gift early. Not if you don't tell anyone."

I didn't think her capable of apologetic gestures, but this, apparently, is one. When I see what she has brought me, I smile for the first time in days. A little fish. A little orange and white fish.

"A ship came in with a whole shoal of them in barrels, live. Well – some of them were live."

I am grinning with wonder. "What do I feed it?"

"I don't know. Bread? Meat? From your own meals, mind. My husband will skin you alive if he sees you

98

wasting food."

"Is it wasting food if…" I dandle my finger in the water. The little fish waggles up to the surface, nipping with a soft mouth. "I'd be taking care of my friend."

"Yes! Yes, it would be wasting food. Silvan, you have to learn not to anger Decimus. You have to learn to be a decent slave."

"Perhaps he should learn not to hit people."

I don't realise what I am saying. The fish is too adorable. She is staring at me with astonishment. Laughter.

We sit together so unconventionally, watching the fish. The household is busy for the coming festivities; I smell hot pastry, flowers, fresh oil in the lamps. Decimus has said nothing of my return. I think he has reconsidered his offer, and I am glad of it. I have never been free and fear I will not catch the knack of it.

"I heard what those Christians said about me, before the funeral," Aurelia says. "It angered my husband. He has long desired children and there have been many false alarms. I think he begins to suspect me of resorting to magic to thwart his seed."

I didn't know this. Her face is overcast, and I dare to touch her hand, as I did when we were small. She permits me.

"Silvan, I am going to have a child."

I smile for her.

"I haven't told him yet. I need you by my side during this early stage. What with the revelries coming soon and the loss of Mother, I must be as serene as possible in order to deliver Decimus a son. Can I count on you? My Silvan? Our secret?"

To think, I almost abandoned her. Devotion without

end.

"Do you remember," Aurelia says, after a time, "when we were little, and Mother would have us act out plays of the gods in masks and cloaks? At the end of the play, you would take off your cloak and say *'The gods are naked; they take nothing, only give'*. Do you recall?"

"I do."

"Decimus is not a god," she says. "He can only take."

ALL TURNS BLACK after this revelation. My visitors continue to come. Some bring damp children, and God forgive me, I ignore them. If I can't hear, I can't care. And if I do care, I can't help, so where's the use in listening? I play the corpse, but my ears refuse to lie dormant.

The voice of a small boy: "Is he dead?"

His mother: "Yes. Well, no. Sort of."

It is a man's turn to speak up. "You can't be sort of dead, love."

"He is a miracle."

With a flourish of relief, I recognise the birdsong of Shelter Girl. I see her approach me, candle in hand. Her clothes, sodden. Something is wrong.

"The blessed martyr Saint Silvan died thousands of years ago," she says. "But last night, he saved my life. Mine, and my husband's."

That certainly beats *Wow, isn't he gorgeous?* Silence from the other visitors while they wonder if this woman might turn violent. Her life, did she say? In my melancholy, I

101

doubt what I am hearing.

"How did he manage that?" says the man. Belatedly, I realise this is Az. It is flagrant flouting of the rules for his type to openly mingle with the living, and he knows it. He rocks there on his heels with his picnic blazer and baby face, casting cheeky looks my way. Shelter Girl's face is ashen.

Her *life?*

"He moved," she says steadily. "I was asleep in my cot in the shelter, and out of nowhere the nightmares stopped. I saw him walking a long passageway. When I woke up, I was out of bed, sleepwalking my way to the back door, and my husband was trying to wake me, but I was distraught. I kept saying, 'Get on the boat', and he asked what boat, and I said 'Illyricone' or 'Illyridom'. A made-up word, anyway. Or something foreign."

Az shrugs. "Illyricum. Old name for Croatia. Terribly old. You probably soaked it up from Tourist Information."

"It doesn't end there. In my dream, Silvan was walking. He was heading for a party. I could hear the music and the pouring of the wine down the corridor. And in the other direction, there was a river. And I said to him, 'Don't go'. And he heard me, and he pointed back towards the river and he said, 'The boat', and I wondered why a saint was talking to me about that bloody banker and his Jolly Jamaican yacht moored outside." She snorts but won't smile, shakes her head, takes a breath. "There are half a dozen rescue cruisers down the hill from the shelter, for picking up stragglers. I was out of my mind, my husband said, running down there in my bare feet, security tearing after me, but I just had to get down that bank, to the nearest boat, a dinghy, the yacht, I didn't give a toss. He had no choice but to jump in after me, into a lifeboat, and then it just–"

She stops. A ripple goes out into the church. They all know something I do not. Something they would rather not name.

In the end, it is Az who speaks:

"The cloudburst."

"It was like the sky had turned into the sea. The Jolly Jamaican capsized like a toy. We saw the shelter roof come down. It was only a prefab. Had we not been on the boat we would have been swept away. Like everyone else."

The mother and child have edged politely away. I lie still, but I feel as though I am shaking. In Cryptspace I had heard nothing of the mortal tragedy above. While I dreamt of a world two-thousand years dead, a fragile living woman I cared about was almost killed.

Az bites his lip, sly in the face of Shelter Girl's fervour.

"Love, I understand you've just survived something traumatic and inexplicable, but this fellow's not sending you any messages. Look at him. It's just one of those things, like soldiers seeing angels on the battlefield."

For a moment, she is stunned. The candle drips wax onto her fingers, but she doesn't move. "You're wrong."

"Get some sleep, eh?"

"Just because you've never experienced anything so–"

"So what? Callous? If he's so holy, why did he not save everyone else?"

"Because I'd come to him for aid before. How else do you explain it?" She drags a hand through her stiff and tangled hair. "And we did save people. Four of them. We did the best we could."

"Oh, four. Out of all those hundreds. So he selectively

rescued you, did he? Pretty shoddy of him, I'd say. Do all those floating bodies not bother him?"

In my glass case, I want to shout. You are hurting her, Az. Stop hurting her.

"I don't care what you call it," she says. "I should be dead. So should my husband."

Az shoves his hands in his pockets. "Lucky for both of you. But luck's all it is."

Her pale brow sweats. She is exhausted, and the strain shows on her whole body. The woman who once laughed at harvest festival clings to the rocks. "I was *there*. You've probably got some mountain mansion with its own generator and a cellar full of food. You don't get what it's like for us from the lowlands. You can't remotely understand life and death when you're cushioned and cynical and–"

"Alriiiight. Lady, I see you're distressed. But this is for your own good. You can't just go around talking about saints giving you warnings in your dreams. They don't canonise mystics anymore. They institutionalise them."

"Shit."

"Excuse you. We're in a church."

"Look," she cries.

"Look at what?"

"He's moved."

"What?"

"He's *moved*."

She points at me. Az is the opposite of dismayed. A smile curls across his face.

"No, he hasn't," he says, though he sees precisely what she does.

"His hand. It's clenched."

"It was clenched earlier."

"No, it was open."

God love her, Shelter Girl is right. I couldn't help it. My right hand, usually limp as a sleeping babe's, has tightened into a fist, and as she drops to her knees before me – in prayer or fright, who knows? – Az stands there, smugly chewing on his thumbnail. He knows I can see him and he knows how serious this is. He provoked me. I have been tricked.

Shelter Girl drops her candle and runs.

I am Miracle once more.

3

"The simulacrum is never that which conceals the truth – it is the truth which conceals that there is none. The simulacrum is true."

– Attributed by philosopher Jean Baudrillard to Ecclesiastes in his 1981 treatise, 'Simulacra and Simulation'. No such Biblical quote exists.

THESE DAYS, MIRACLES are placed under house arrest. No sooner has Shelter Girl gone out shouting into the streets, someone calls the police. Someone notifies the television stations. Someone, presumably, has sent a dinghy out to bother the Pope. *Sole Survivors Saved By Sleeping Saint.*

It would normally be a novelty headline, but the tragedy of the cloudburst has broken people's last tendons of resolve and they yearn for comfort. Candles and flowers pile up at my altar. My clownfish is taken from me, like evidence from a crime scene. People pose for photographs on their knees beside my miraculously transformed hand. By noon the crowds are surging. Someone shouts at the laywomen to lift me out of my bower, to let the people touch me, kiss me, liberate a lock of hair...

It is too much, and they close the church.

Yet the people gather outside, weeping hopeful tears. Someone plays a saxophone, like the call of a mournful bird.

God is coming, it seems to say.

But I am not God.

"If you wanted to really cause a stir, you could put one leg in the air."

"Go away, Az."

It is not Az. I open my eyes to the stiff green sight of Mister Lenin.

"You are fatigued," he says, and graciously helps me climb out of my bower.

"The cameramen dropped chewing gum all down the aisle. People started cutting up the chair cushions to sell as relics. We're not prepared for this sort of thing here. I've caused the laywomen no end of trouble. What news of Shelter Girl?"

"Your young woman has been taken in by the Church committee. They are analysing her."

That means something different with every passing century. I could already hear the snide interrogation: *Have you seen Jesus in your toast recently?* Still, I'd rather she suffer that than the rack.

"I wouldn't be concerned," Lenin tells me. "This way, she and her husband will receive the best care and counselling available, particularly if she intrigues them with her story."

I look at him, astonished. If?

"Crying Madonnas have a way of weeping cooking oil," he explains. "Levitating gurus conceal their perches in their robes. It's a hard world to fool, these days. That said, your friends Thérèse and Bernadette are enjoying the reflected glow of your newfound fame. The usual lunatics say the End Times grow near, that the Virgin will come for the righteous before the angel passes over with his sword. Nightly vigils at shrines and churches, all over the world. It is not unlike revolution, what you've done. If tainted with superstition."

I cannot call on any of my fellow Miracles, not while we are watched so closely. I am alone. "Is Valerius safe?"

He huffs. "Oh, yes. With his tattooed devotees in their leather jackets. Valerius is a novelty. Old bones. But you? With this face, you have moved people. The things I had to do to whip up this kind of fervour in my time! You are breathing new life into this dead religion. As a philosopher once said, *'The tyrant dies and his rule is over; the martyr dies and his rule begins'*."

Coming down the steps from the altar, I tread on photographs and letters like fallen leaves. *Blessed Martyr, pray for Michael, lost at sea. Pray for Elaine. Pray for Jimmy.* Who do they think I am?

"I am a lowly slave, Mister Lenin."

"Must it remain that way?"

Outside, the pilgrims are singing, *Lord have mercy upon us, Christ have mercy upon us.* I wish again to be struck down deaf, but mercy does not come. Instead, an idea arises. I hurry to the crypt, neglecting to even say goodbye to my visitor. When fretful Johann greets me, I pull him into my arms as if I will never see him again. I fly into the rose-scented tunnels, past Delaroche, past Millais, past Leonardo, past the overflowing streams, soupy-thick with Coke bottles and supermarket carrier bags – how am I only noticing that now? I do not look back for Mister Lenin, and I am glad. I wouldn't have liked the flash of his teeth as they severed the green tip of his thumb.

FLORENCE. BEAUTIFUL CITY. Where else can I go?

"I've brought you a gift. It isn't makeup."

Venus likes gifts. I remember her saying so. She idles in her glass case, like a cat interrupted at sleep, only this cat is sleeping in a puddle of her own innards, and I still cannot view her without that old religious horror. I cannot conceive of someone laid out like this, so gorily, if spiritual rapture is not the aim. Are you sure you were not martyred, I want to ask? You'd be surprised what you can forget.

I produce Johann's music machine from my tunic and attach it to the set of tiny speakers I managed to lift from him during our embrace. A wail goes out into the chamber; a ringing, singing, round sound, and Venus reaches out with her slender hand and opens her case to the kiss of the music.

"Oh," she sighs with her splayed yellow lungs. "*Oh.*"

"It's you. The song of the planet Venus."

I sit at her side and press my forehead to my knees.

I tell her everything. Like a saint, she listens without

interruption, merely batting her long eyelashes as I gush like a faulty drain. It keeps bubbling out, that word, 'slave'. Against the yearning howl of the planet Venus it feels small in my mouth.

"That sound," she says when I am finished. "That music, it was… vast. It made me want… I don't know. To peel off the roof and look at the stars."

"To book a flight and visit one?" I suggest. My heart isn't in it.

"Yes! Too late for fuel conservation now. Hmm. To visit the stars. You know, I never thought all that talk of the music of the spheres would turn out to be true. Signor Sarti had the most poetic way of speaking, particularly when the gentlemen came to see me. He was like a loving father, the way he pulled me apart and put me back together. I think about him sometimes. Where he is now, whether he loves his creation still. Not like your master. He sounds a very devil. I don't blame you, trying to forget him."

I stare up at her, queenly in her raiment of pearls and flesh. "What is it like for you, lying here, being looked at? Don't you ever feel useless?"

The question has never occurred to her. "Bored, more like. When you've travelled a continent as the headline act, being locked in a museum isn't exactly a thrill." She takes her long braid and smoothes it over her shoulder. "But I'm created to fulfil a human need. I give a glimpse of death without loss. I am lifelike, yet subject to no earthly putrefaction…"

"Yes!" I interrupt. "We are the same." It is rude, but she forgives me with her lovely smile. I would blush if my blood still flowed.

"Signor Sarti once said that the human form is a

miniature universe. As Mother Earth must be broken apart to give up her secrets, so must a beautiful body. That's why I look the way I do, like a sleeping maiden. Man's desire to look, to touch, to tear open… it extends to the Earth and a helpless girl alike. So long as they may get away with it."

I think of Az and his talk of Hell. But then I think of the living world with its rumbling clouds and the rain that tastes of vinegar. On a long enough timescale, Man never really gets away with anything.

"But it's all so terrible to me. The only time a person sees the inside of another is at a time of tragedy, or war. God made our faces in his beautiful image. Not our guts and our filth. This is… it's almost…" I am clumsy with confusion. "Evil."

If she is hurt, she doesn't show it. "I teach physicians," she says, patiently. "My visitors queue to gaze upon my viscera, but that doesn't mean they've come to denounce the magic of the human machine. Quite the opposite. They don't look at me to be reminded of death. They look at me to learn more about the wonder of living."

With this, she hefts the skirt of her intestines. I expect them to give a merry frou-frou ruffle, but they do not move at all.

I stand and look about me at the jars of floating matter. Parts of people long passed, arrested in time for the eyes of the living. "But my visitors come, and they see my blood, and wound. The death of me."

She laughs. "Yes, but it's different, isn't it?"

"How?"

"We're not the same as them," she says. "So it doesn't scare them."

"But I have a body, like they do. And it bled, like

theirs do."

She playfully swats my hand. "You mustn't pretend to be stupid. One can be clever and gorgeous at the same time, you know."

"I don't understand you, Venus."

"You must get over this silly shyness. Look, try this." Before I can dart out of the way, she's taken hold of my wrist and is poking my finger into the packed collection of mottled shapes that make up her inner cavity, and I flinch, expecting warm mush, but...

"It's... hard."

"Give it a tap," she says.

I flick her left lung with my fingertip. It is like tapping a candle.

"I am made of wax, Silvan."

My jaw trembles. I try to jerk my hand away, but she holds it there, staring kindly into my stricken face. "But you are... You have a..."

"A human body? You're so *sweet*. I'm a copy of a human body, Silvan. A simulacrum. Cadavers are messy and come with all sorts of ethical qualms. I am clean and lovely. Like you."

Like me.

"Wax," I whisper.

I take the pin from my cloak and it falls to the floor in a red torrent. I dig the pin into my left hand, the soft palm. At first, nothing happens, and so I apply more pressure. A crack appears. I think of fortune tellers and life lines. I push harder, a prising motion, and the crack deepens until there is no more doubt about the meaning of the line. My flesh crumbles into fragments and I tip my palm to watch them trickle to the floor.

Know thyself, says Signor Sarti's sign. *Know thyself.*

114

I KNOW I am not wax, because when I fall into my memories once more, I am bleeding. I come to holding a broken jar of wine, two jagged fragments in the cup of my palms, squatting down on the mosaic floor of Decimus and Aurelia's villa. Felix, one of the household's youngest slaves, has dropped the jar and is panting with terror at what the master will say. As a Gaul newly captured and sold, he speaks little Latin. Probably for the best – he doesn't know his new name means 'lucky'.

"Don't worry," I tell him, despite my cut finger. "It's Saturnalia. You are not the servant today. You are served."

He plainly suspects there's a catch. I pat his head.

"Try to have some fun."

Everyone else is, it seems. Cornelius, the gardener, has been crowned the King of Saturnalia and sits on a gaudy throne, commanding his colleagues to dance and drink and throw off their clothes. We must obey him; that is the only rule. Aurelia, dressed in the simple smock of a plebeian, doles out wine to her slaves, smiling as she

115

plays along with their haughty demands. Even Decimus is here, wearing the uniform of a common cavalry soldier, pinching the slave girls' bottoms and asking if they'd like to ride his stallion. There is a rumour he has spiked the wine with mandrake. Judging from all the kissing and writhing and raucous laughter, I suspect the rumour is true. I don't let a drop pass my lips.

Aurelia lurches to the corner of the room to be sick. I rush to her, keeping her hair out of the way as she bends and retches.

"You've been a naughty slave, Aurelia," I tease her. "Too much wine on the job."

She wipes her mouth and grins at me.

"I always get like this," she says. "It means the baby is alive."

The little Gaul boy comes over with a mop and bucket. "I clean?"

"It's alright, Felix. I'll take care of it. Go and eat something."

I hear the call of my master over the hubbub and music. "Is that a slave I spy, slaving? What does the King make of that?"

On his throne, Cornelius waves his felt crown and bellows, "Forfeit!"

Felix cringes at the sound. The rest of the household hammer on the tables and stamp their feet. "Forfeit! Forfeit!"

Decimus, none too steady, crosses the room to us. Little Felix looks to me with panic in his eyes. For all the pretence of switching roles for the night, Decimus still carries his vitis staff, swishing it through the air for the satisfying noise.

"No respect for tradition, that's the problem with

Gauls. And you, Silvan – whatever it is that you are. Can't follow a simple command, eh?"

Aurelia puts herself between us. "Slaves are naturally slavish. They can't help it. Why don't I pour you another drink?"

"You've been sick."

"Too much wine, love."

In the lamplight his pupils are black mirrors. "You are never sick."

The revellers are still chanting 'forfeit', at war with the deafening drums and whistling flutes. Annoyed that the attention has shifted from him, Cornelius hurls a goblet across the room and laughs as it smashes against a pillar.

"The King," he shrieks, "demands satisfaction. Felix! Boy. Come to me."

Felix understands the beckoning gesture, but not the words. I know how this usually goes. Any slave not fully invested in the festivities is branded a spoilsport and must do something mildly humiliating – sing a song naked, or beg like a dog for a scrap of meat. Head bowed, Felix approaches the throne where Cornelius bids him kneel. Decimus is still eyeing his wife's vomit. The drugged wine has sharpened his mistrust but dulled his wits, and I see him struggling to come to a conclusion.

"You are never sick," he repeats slowly. "Except when you are with child."

Aurelia places both hands on his chest and attempts to steer him back to the party. "Come, husband, the King is waiting. What will he have Felix do? I say we chase him around the gardens. If we catch him before he reaches the ponds, we can tickle him with feathers until he cries for mercy."

"You are never... sick. Except..." The vitis staff

falters, mid-air. "Why would you keep this from me?"

"Not here, husband. We will talk later."

He shoves her from him, and some of the slaves unwisely decide to boo. "You will talk whenever I wish it," Decimus says. Changing his mind, he grabs her by the shoulders and hauls her against his chest, feeling for the slight curve of her middle. "You did not tell me. It's true. And you did not tell me."

Felix watches all this with incomprehension and dread. I can't blame him. I stand behind Aurelia, knowing my master's temper. If he strikes her, I must prevent a fall.

"What else do you keep from me, Aurelia?"

Aurelia has wedged a protective hand between them. "I had to be sure. I did not want to give false hope."

"The King is waiting, soldier!" Cornelius shouts, apparently too drunk to gauge the severity of Decimus' mood.

But my master lets go of his wife, swinging on his heel to approach the throne. "I ask the King of Saturnalia to grant me a wish," he says cheerfully.

"What wish is this?"

"This slave, Felix, has insulted the gods, refusing to abandon his subservient habits when commanded to. I wish to punish him."

"And what punishment do you have in mind?" crows the King. He is hoping for the naked singing option. We all know what Cornelius thinks of hairless young boys. On his knees, Felix dares to glance up at his master. *Is this a game?* his eyes seem to ask.

"Put your hands on the floor," says Decimus, miming. "Like a dog."

This much Felix understands. With relief, he takes the

118

pose of a submissive hound, rear in the air, head tilted up. Nervous chuckles ripple out around him. His lips form a tentative ring, and at Cornelius' coaxing, he gives a thin, high howl, causing eruptions all over the room. Even Decimus laughs.

The laughter is short-lived. Decimus stamps. First Felix's right hand, flat against the stone, and then the left. Decimus rams his boot down as if trying to break thick ice. I hear the crunch of bone-twigs. When the realisation of what is happening belatedly floods Felix's brain, he screams us much in shock as in pain as Decimus's foot comes heavily down again and again. The howl of a dog morphs into a noise all too human, and the mandrake in the wine has everyone cackling hysterically at the amusing turn of events. The smell of blood is hot honey to them, and more than one tongue peeks out to taste the air.

"Not so lucky now, Felix!" the King is shrieking, as Felix curls into a shuddering, bleeding ball. "Not so lucky now!"

Sated, Decimus stretches the kinks from his shoulders. He nudges Felix with his boot, the leather dark with blood. "Get me some wine, boy. Woof. Get your master some wine."

I go to fetch a jar in Felix's stead, but Aurelia has a fistful of my tunic.

"Don't," she mutters.

Felix cannot rise. Decimus turns to his audience, arms wide in mock exasperation. "The world has indeed turned on its head. My slave will not fetch me libation. My wife will not tell me she carries my child. If I were a suspicious man—"

He shoots a look over his shoulder then, in Aurelia's

direction. No doubt it is a half-threat, gussied up in the irony of the festivities, but he catches her with her hand bunched in my tunic, the meagre puddle of vomit behind us like a filthy secret, and the siege engine of his brain chugs into motion.

I remember it all, now.

"Prove it."

Aurelia, smiling stiffly: "My love?"

"Your wifely obedience. Prove it."

Even the most inebriated among us cringes to see our superiors bickering like old women at the forum. *Bring back the entertainment,* I can almost hear them wishing. *Tread on Felix again.* But Felix is using his elbows to drag his carcass to a safe corner, trailing blood and fingernails, and Decimus' attention is focused most definitely on Aurelia. And me.

"Prove to me that whelp inside you comes from your husband."

I'm not certain of the exact moment she lets go of me. Only that she makes quick and lively steps in Decimus' direction and leaves me with her puddle. He is a statue then, like one of the many marble likenesses of the Divine Emperor around the city. They all look so proud, those statues, though everyone knows the bodies are recycled Emperors from generations ago, the heads merely screwed on, waiting to be replaced. Secretly, they make me laugh, those statues. If a man is divine – eternal as the very rocks! – why stoop to saying so in public? But that is what I see in Decimus' eyes now: desperation, small and mean.

"Prove it," he says. "Prove it."

Aurelia attempts to take his arm. "Why don't we adjourn to our private rooms? Leave these people to their feasting? Hm?"

"He comes too."

Neither of them have to look at me. Like poor Felix, I know a dead end when I see one.

"Him? What use have I for a lapdog, my love? I tire of playing the slave. Let us retire for the night, and celebrate our good fortune. Yes?"

"He. Comes. Too."

My mistress submits. When Decimus turns to leave, she downs a whole glass of wine.

It's an interesting drug, mandrake. Best grown in soil where blood is spilled, in small doses it will ease pain and usher in prophetic dreams from the gods. Added to alcohol, it kindles lust and makes one want to leap and dance. Colours sing, objects seem to swell and ebb in time with the heartbeat, and feelings of confidence spring from a seemingly bottomless well within. Take enough mandrake, and you will feel immortal. Take too much, and you will die.

Decimus, I am sorry to say, has not tipped the balance. One prevailing Roman talent is to indulge in excess without looking like you're indulging in excess. Only barbarians drink too much or eat until it hurts to walk. Romans are merely convivial.

And so I follow my convivial master and silently panicking mistress down the hall and away from Saturnalia. I can still hear the King over the racing drums, laughing at Felix. The boy is no good to anyone now. In my anxiety, I haven't noticed we have long since passed the elegant living areas of the villa and travelled down to the slave quarters. Decimus is moving like a man with fire for feet.

"It occurs to me, Silvan..." he shouts over his

shoulder as Aurelia and I struggle to keep up. "In keeping with the spirit of the season, it ought to be you who plays host."

"Wouldn't you rather be comfortable? His room will be depressing." Aurelia manages a merry little laugh before finding herself pinned to the wall by the wrists.

Decimus leers into her face. "Intimate with the contents of his room, are you?"

Aurelia's cheeks are flushed with wine, but still her eyes are clever. "No, love. A slave wouldn't know what to do with a lavish chamber. He probably thinks a straw mattress is overwhelmingly grand. Let us go and enjoy the garden. Smell the jasmine."

"I would see his room."

I can see his face in the dark moons of her pupils. She looks to me as casually as she may. I cannot think why she wants to keep him from my room, what offence he may find there.

"My room is damp this time of year," I offer. "Perhaps my lady would be better suited—"

It's eerie when someone pretends not to have heard you speak. More so when one finds a knife niggling the small of one's back.

And so I open my room to my superiors.

My clownfish circles. He rises to the surface when I come near, blowing me kisses in case I have breadcrumbs. A bed, a chest, some blankets, and a ceiling shadowed with last week's rain. This is my life.

Decimus closes the door upon us. I think of my boyhood with Aurelia, the games we would play; she, the queen of an imaginary land, and I, her devoted swain. I remember our trips to the temple, Aurelia tugging my hair and threatening to sacrifice me to the gods. When

Mother clipped her ear for being disrespectful, she retorted, "Well, you're not supposed to sacrifice something you don't want, are you?"

None of us sit. Aurelia's hand flutters at womb-level. Her brow shines with perspiration. When I go to fetch her a glass of water, Decimus sweeps into my path like a marauding ship and I am forced backwards into the wall.

"You could have been in Illyricum by now. How does it feel? To think of that ship shrinking to nothing on the horizon?"

Past the trunk of his bicep, I see the hurt on Aurelia's face and feel a swell of guilt.

"She knows," he says. "We had our disagreements on the subject, but where was the point in arguing? She saw you that night, aching to leave. Cruel of you, considering."

It is meant to mean something, and I don't know what, but he glances to her with her hand on her belly and my mouth falls open.

"No," Aurelia grits.

"No?" he says.

"*No.*"

He turns to me. "Prove it."

She is coughing or laughing. Her dress is patched with sweat, and the hand at her middle trembles. She needs to sit down, but there is a rigidity about her that worries me. The vein at her temple. Belatedly, I remember the mandrake and fear for the child.

Decimus' breastplate is flush with my own chest. My breathing intensifies as he leans in, constricting my ribs. "You had your opportunity to leave," he tells me, as finally as if I have signed a contract.

At last Aurelia finds her voice. "I have committed no

impropriety. How could I? We grew up together."

"That always bothered me. What kind of a woman claims kinship with a slave? The same kind of woman who presents an inferior with gifts? Pet fish," he sneers. "They talk about you in the kitchens, woman. Yes. And the forums, and the barracks. My men make merry at the thought of their captain's wife and her generous spirit."

He grinds out all of this into my face, the veins in his eyes broken gutters of red, and I see the danger then, see it plainly. Livid, beautiful fate.

Or perhaps that's hindsight.

He doesn't need to state his demands of her. He doesn't need to slap her, either, but he is shaking with the mandrake and the full-circle swing of his body seems to satisfy some ache. I go to her without thinking, but run straight into his hands and am lifted, pinned, scrambling with fingernails where his hand squeezes my throat.

"Prove it, Aurelia."

His hands are the perfect size for my neck. Aurelia's high, keening sounds do nothing to distract him from his purpose, biceps bunching, lifting me. The tips of my toes kiss the tiles. My body convulses: the pretty thing born for service, for the enjoyment of others. It thrashes in search of air, and somewhere inside Decimus' chest there is a rumbling noise, a pleased noise, and he opens his hand just slightly, enough for the stars to retreat to the corners of my eyes and the ringing noise to quieten.

"What a colour he is."

"Beautiful," Aurelia says. In a white haze, I see her rise behind him, his knife grinning in her fist. I see the room in fragments as consciousness stutters. Decimus is putting me down. Decimus is loosening his grip on my throat. Decimus is making the sounds he does when in rut. I think for a fragment of a second she has penetrated him with his own knife, that her old love for me somehow suddenly equals my own thick-headed devotion and she will save me from the tortures my master is entitled to put me through.

I am falling.

She tells him she loves him.

She goes about proving it.

You mustn't listen to the naysayers. There is no such thing as true oblivion. I know, not because I am Miracle, but because despite almost two-thousand years of willing it otherwise, I recall the signature of each bruise, the song of their sandals on the tiles, and the wine in their sweat, blow by blow by blow by blow.

"We should slit the corners of his mouth." Aurelia wheezes through her teeth as she kicks me. "Make him smile."

"Aurelia, my love." And they laugh.

"We will have a son."

I am hoisted. Copper in my mouth. My clownfish circles his glass Universe and feels no dread. For that, I am thankful. One may spend a lifetime nurturing the thorns of betrayal, crying out for those who abandoned you and made you bleed. It's a tiring way to live. Say what you like about death and the meaning of it, but it has a way of casting out the poison in the blood.

Ribs fail me like rotten rafters. I taste loose teeth. I raise my eyes to my sister and see a stranger. Nevertheless, I tell myself, a stranger who hasn't a choice.

Or is that hindsight again?

Perhaps it isn't meant to go any further. My master, at least, is beginning to tire, and the furious red print of his hand on Aurelia's face will be hard to explain. But Aurelia lunges. Hear it: the high, undignified shriek of a man who isn't me. I slide to the tiles where it is cool and lovely, but my peace is shattered by the cries of my master, his outraged howls as the blood flows from his hand, clutched to his chest.

"Bitch! Idiot bitch!"

She had made to slash me, my Aurelia, my sister in name only; to ruin my valuable face and thus clear her name. But Decimus, eager to crush my throat once more, had moved too fast, placed his thumb in the path of the driving blade. The ruby tip lies at my feet, thumbnail attached. She does so love the sight of blood, Aurelia. But she is not happy, not even so much as tickled, now, as the magic of the wine wears off and breath comes fast and hard. She catches his fist with her cheek, and she is on the floor with me, spluttering crude denials, something about sons, streams of sons, and I think to myself...

Who will look after my fish?

There is a damp patch on the ceiling. The December rain is seeping in. The knife in Aurelia's hand enters my throat and life leaves me in a flood.

VENUS LIES AT my side on the museum floor. Her cold hand has come to rest on my own and I stare numbly down into the open hollow of her body.

"Such an ugly waste," she says.

"They all tell me I was a martyr." I look her in the eye and say it: "Venus, I have been lying to people."

We lie together on my discarded cloak, a pool of red against the marble, scattered with the chunks of wax I have picked from my hand.

"There are slices of liver down the hall taken from an unclaimed transient man," she says. "'Teaching aids', the label says. I call him Brian. Perhaps he was a Steven or a Cassius, but where's the harm in it, indulging in a little humanity? So you're not a martyr. You are still Silvan. The boy in fancy dress who brought me lipstick."

She smiles. Perhaps it is the shock of my discovery, but she is lovelier now than ever before, this flayed horror of a girl, and it brings me back into my body. I have forgotten the sensation of another person at one's side without the demanding entreaty of prayer.

But she is not a body. She is wax.

"Venus, I was incorrupt. I was Miracle. This is obscene."

I hold up my ruined hand.

"That is a hand," she says gently. She holds it open for us both to see, the flesh-coloured wax crumbling to reveal the grey stone of my skeleton. "This is a metacarpal bone. And this, here, is a proximal phalange. If we were to peel this back, towards the wrist, you would see your little carpals, like pebbles. And then your long radius, and your ulna. Yours are fine bones. Your people are right to marvel at you."

I close my eyes and take back my hand. "Please don't praise me."

As I stand and turn my back, I see her reaching for me. "Why? You're being silly again."

Silly is wanting to visit distant planets. Silly is thinking a touch of makeup is Divine.

"Silvan, don't go away. What you said about the stars… about the music of the spheres… I want that. I want to see life again. I don't care what you're not. Come back someday, won't you? When you're feeling better." As I near the exit, I hear her sigh. "No one else talks to me."

Az always manages to appear when I'd rather be alone. He swings around a Cryptspace lamppost, practically Fred Astaire with his beaming white teeth and foxtrot feet.

"Going to see Mister Lenin?" he calls out.

"I can't." I say it to the stones. He doesn't hear me.

"Did you know he gets a new silk suit once every three years? It's alright for some." He falls into step with me, an arm around my shoulder. "What's up, buttercup?"

"Az, he was right. I am not Miracle."

I show him my hand. The old bones within. I wish I could remember their names. Venus made them somehow sound poetic, despite the pain they're causing me. Bones where the magic of God ought to be. Just bones.

His cheery face falls. "Oh, sweetiepie," he says. "Oh, what a pickle you're in."

"And all those people, outside the church, singing…" I could cry, if I had tear ducts. At the sight of his sympathetic eyes, the wave building inside me crests. "Az, you could help me. You were an angel once, weren't you? Do you still have wings? You could take me somewhere. A mountain summit. You could bury me there, under the snow, where no one will find me. Or a volcano. Yes! Fly me over a volcano and let me drop. Wax melts. I can get rid of the lie, Az."

As I am fantasising, my hands flutter, and he takes hold of them and lifts them to his lips, warming them with his breath. He leads me to a nook under a painting of Saint Denis and his miraculous decapitation. The story goes, Denis met a bunch of French pagans in 240AD, and subsequently lost his head. He proceeded to walk six kilometres with it tucked under his arm, preaching all the way, apart from a brief pause to rinse the head in a stream. He's now the Patron Saint of hydrophobia, hilariously enough.

People will believe anything.

There is a stone bench to perch on, and Az wipes it dry for me with his handkerchief.

"Come on, now," he tells me. "How many splinters of the True Cross are a sham? How hard would it be to knock up a few copies of the Turin Shroud with a bit of soy sauce and some dirty muslin? And I have it on good authority, actually, that your friend Deodatus' skull is that of a young *woman*. Very few differences between a male and female skull, you know. Less so to some sixteenth-century cleric trying to drum up a quick buck—"

"Stop it."

"Deodatus is a generic Latin name. It's like calling someone Saint Fred. I was there, that's what they did. When the Reformation knocked them for six, the Catholics raided Roman cemeteries for interesting bones and declared them saints. They shipped them off all over

Europe to lure those pilgrim purses. When they ran out of names, they just gave up. Saint Anon, Saint Incognitus… Saint Doodah-Whatshisname. And at one point, some Swiss scallywag tried to pass off a pumice stone as Saint Peter's calcified brain. Look it up. So, you know. Could be worse."

His nonchalance makes me frantic. I thrust my ruined hand at him. "This doesn't disturb you?"

"Darling, I've perched on dying icecaps and popped a chunk in my drink. I've shaken hands with oil barons and sat on Presidents' knees while they clog Arab skies with their great big orphan-making bombers. Your pretty little fingerbones don't scare me."

He puts his arm around me. His flesh is supple against unyielding wax. It is good, I register distantly. He is good. But the adoration of inanimate objects is idolatry and I push him away for his own safety.

Still, he chucks my chin as if I were a baby. "So you're no saint. What does it matter? If anyone cared, they'd have done something about it by now." He winds a Da Vinci finger up through the air, indicating the heavens. "Know what I mean?"

I know what he means, and I watch the water passing us by. "All this attention," I murmur. "All those poor people and their desperate sincerity. And I, nothing but a doll."

Az scoffs. "It's a bit late for desperation. If their grandparents had been up for a bit of Lenten self-sacrifice a few hundred years ago, we wouldn't be in this watery mess. But no, mamma's gotta have her 4x4; how else are the kids supposed to get to school, half a mile away? Humans. I know you're not supposed to say this stuff out loud, but I bloody hate them. Not just sometimes. It's a habit I can't get rid of."

I open my mouth to give some mild reproach, but he's in full swing.

"They want forgiving, those people outside your church. But look what they did to Shelter Girl. She was a queen to that tribe of eco-freaks. She and her hubbie pulled them together and kept them safe so they could offer a few tiny acts of kindness to this ravaged Earth. And what did the locals do? When they saw all those tents, they had the police come and rip them down. They trashed the beehives, confiscated the food. Disgrace. Infamy."

"What do you know about Shelter Girl?"

"I watch. She's a toughie. Not many figureheads like her left, let me tell you. No, that lot out there singing Kumbayah, they're all about the cash and the comforts and the *me-first-me-first*, but when they paint themselves into a corner with their greed and their bastardry, they come limping back to the likes of you and me and the Good Lord for a pat on the head so they can wipe the slate clean and start again. Peasants."

He is up now, pacing, petite and pretty, and I have to remind myself once more of what he is. Perhaps, if I am talking to an angel, it isn't all bunk.

But Az is not that kind of angel.

He whirls on his heel, a smile on his face like a picnic in summer. "Come with me. This whole stinking world will be underwater by Christmas. But you and me, we don't need air to breathe. We can dive into Paris. Shack up in the catacombs. We can swim up the *Tour Eiffel* and I'll smash Chanel's windows and fetch you a crown of deep-sea pearls. You'd like that, wouldn't you? Someone serving you for a change."

He kneels at my feet and I do my best not to draw back, but I am undeserving, and my words come out bitterly. "Dolls are for dressing."

His eyes are unexpectedly sincere. "One like you should never be a slave."

"No? Says who? The same person who said those people should drown, seeking shelter?"

The eyes twinkle. "You're beginning to sound like me."

We sit companionably in silence; I, staring at my hand, and he at me, daring once to brush the hair from my eyes, frowning at the sadness he sees there. He rummages for something in his pocket, something bird-bone fragile, and with a twirl of his delicate fingers, I find he has placed a crown upon my head. A coronet of the finest golden filigree.

I take the crown and turn it in my hands. "This belongs to Valerius."

"Not anymore. Wear it. It's made for one as lovely as you, not some Halloween fright." He adds softly, "You shouldn't be anyone's servant. Not even God's."

Thérèse always told me I wasn't very bright. I am wrung out from the shocks of the past few days, and, as it turns out, not in possession of a human brain. But as I stare at Valerius' crown there are questions beyond my capabilities whispering in my ear. I feel an unsaintly wariness. Something is amiss.

"Promise me," Az says. "When Croatia goes under, you'll come with me. Let the faithful freak out in the meantime. Give them the usual inanimate show. But when it's over, drop them. Drop everyone but yourself. And me."

He doesn't understand. I have to know how I became

this. How did a murdered slave – not even a Christian one – end up here?

But he is right. Croatia will go under. My bower in Saint Blaise's will succumb, the glass crack and the velvet rot. Even the luxurious roiling rose-scent of Cryptspace cannot beautify the miserable flow of rainwater carrying the odd mortal bagatelle past our feet now; a child's plastic boat, dead currency, empty crisp packets. I see Az's point. The nations of the Earth had plenty of time to care about the rainforests and the oil reserves and the plight of the dying pollinators. It will make precious little difference when I get up and leave them.

Az's hand is on my knee, caressing the painted hairless skin. "Don't look so glum," he soothes me. "I've got you. I've had you for so, so long."

The little seducer, he rocks on his heels at my feet. It strikes me in the chest. "It's all been you," I realise.

"What?" He bites his pillowy lip. He is many things, but a straight-up, shark-eyed liar he is not.

"It's you. Everything. You."

I pinch his soft cheek and he squeals. "Not very bloody saintly of you!"

But the guilt glows on his face like rouge.

"What do you mean, you've 'had me'?" I ask.

"Dunno."

"Tell me."

"Shan't."

"You do know!"

"I never expected–" he says. "I never intended–"

I have been had. Thérèse was right. You little fool, Silvan, consorting with devils. Sucking the life out of age-old faith.

"You never intended for me to find out? What I am?"

"Oh, no. No, that I wanted all along."

I am mesmerising to him, standing over him, a crown on my head and a wound in my neck, and just once I wish I could be taken seriously as a man. Perhaps not the man they think I am, but a man who lived, nonetheless. This endless adoration is nothing but draining.

Still he gazes up at me. "Wouldn't you rather know the truth? That's what all those pilgrims want, isn't it? Or what they think they want. Makeup for incorruptible bodies? Come *on*, Silvan. It was dodgy from the get-go. If you didn't want to get toyed with, you'd have made enquiries."

"I was at peace."

"You were ignorant. It's not the same." He comes to me then, full of remorse. "Silvan. You deserve freedom. I meant what I said about Paris. I've been waiting. I've had it all figured out since the fourth century, and I—"

"When I told Valerius your name, he was alarmed." I whisper it to myself, but his guilty dog look only intensifies and my chest fills up with dread. "Who are you?"

He laughs. "Me? Nobody. The Catholic Church issued an edict, didn't you hear? All Apocryphal angels are banished from the canon. You don't know The Book of Enoch, being not actually a Christian. According to the Pope, I don't exist."

He has grown taller, now, and lost the baby fat. I find myself facing a genderless bare-chested splendour heavy with oily chains and perfume to rival the gardens of Babylon. Lips the blue of clouds fit to burst. Good job I am held together with wax – my bones could willingly crumble to dust at the sight of a thing such as him.

Even his voice changes, dropping to a sonorous croon.

"They called me Azazel. '*Azazel, who hath taught all unrighteousness on earth and revealed the eternal secrets which were in heaven. Azazel, who taught men to make swords and knives and shields and breastplates; and bracelets and ornaments; and the use of antimony and the beautifying of the flesh; and all kinds of costly stones and all colouring tinctures. And there arose much godlessness, and men were led astray and became corrupt in all their ways*'. The daughters of Man still cover their heads at prayer, so charmed am I by a head of luscious long hair. God didn't do you justice, I tell them. I can make you miraculous."

The talons on his feet gouge trenches in the flagstones. On the wall behind him, Caravaggio's naked assassin wrestles Saint Matthew, their painted flesh sweltering in Az's reflected heat. Well, I tell myself, this is the end. He's going to smash you like a dribbling candle and melt you down for lipstick. I should have stayed with Venus. I liked her. I should have told her that. People like to be told they're cared for.

"Nigh on two-thousand years I've watched over you," Az goes on. "They lost their nerve when the mandrake wore off, your Roman masters. The murder of a slave is still a murder, so they dragged you into the streets, leaking the whole way with your fetching red juices. I followed the trail, just as I'd followed you since the day you were lifted onto the block to be sold. I stood in the dark with your blood on my toes and I listened. 'They'll say he was robbed,' Decimus said. Aurelia didn't speak at all. Regret's for the sober. They dropped you down a backstreet, in the clay dust. What's that line, in Isaiah? 57:2 − '*And they will rest in their beds*'."

Shelter Girl was right. On my back in the road, a prey animal splayed for the scavenging.

"Did Aurelia have her baby?" I manage to croak.

He blows a peacock lock of hair from his eyes. "Oh, God, no. No, she lost it, and he chucked her down the stairs. Humans. What can you do?"

Grief is a knife. I am on the floor. But he isn't finished, batting those spiked black lashes at me.

"The Christians found you the following dawn. Red Beard and his friends. You were so serene in death. Not some hairy old man with his tongue missing like bishop Romanus. You were a tragedy. You were desirable. *Valuable* is what you were, sweetie pie. You were the martyr they needed. And you weren't there to say otherwise.

"They washed you and they dressed you and they loved every inch of you. Death worshippers, Aurelia said, didn't she? They came from all over to look at you, to touch you and kiss you and stick their fingers in your wound like Doubting Thomas, and it was *thrilling* to them. And I sat with you and held your hand and when things got nasty, three days in, they burned bales of lavender so the visitors could still come and tell you what a perfect angel you were. They had to paint your poor darkening face so the morbid fuckers would still pay to see you. A few days were all they needed anyway. The proclamation went out across the land. The Christian Emperor Constantine heard of you, but by then it was too late, they'd buried you. Had to. But it gave them time. A golden box, a box of such magnificence, the infant Christ could keep his nappies in it. Money for old bones. Incorrupt? Well, it's a flexible term, isn't it? Your bones were still pretty, and Red Beard may have told one or two people they had healing powers. Wouldn't hurt, would it? And it paid for protection. Paid for a church.

And another. And when Red Beard died, it paid for his friends' passage to Greece where they set up a-*nother* church. And all the while, the stories about the boy in the box grew – how he was the most beautiful, the most faithful, the most utterly superlative of them all.

"I followed you for centuries while you slept, so tired of people you couldn't even pick up your little soul and go trotting home to Heaven. I followed you into the nineteenth century when a young modellist in Tuscany came upon an opportunity to make his artistic talents pay. The priests had the relics, but they needed the pilgrims. Pilgrims vomit cash, providing you give them something astonishing. I put the ideas in his head, just a little whisper. *'Slim and slight, Signor Sarti, like Donatello's bronze David'*, and he got to work around your bones with respect. I mean real respect, the kind you'd never got in life or death. Later on, when he was the famous anatomist, exhibiting his gorgeous dead ladies in all the capitals of Europe he'd say *'Know thyself – know the wonderful structure of the human frame'*. He learnt that from you; the exquisite ideal. You've got the kind of bones the scientists call 'gracile'. In a state of lovely grace."

His head brushes the ceiling and the stream rushes as if to escape. He is barefoot and savage with bells on his ankles, and I am too frightened to move.

"And so Signor Sarti bound your bones in wax, encasing them in the body of a sweet and sleeping youth, to lie forever on a bed of velvet in your very own Rome. It was me who made them move you to Croatia in 1847. Illyricum, yes? The safe yellow hills. You wouldn't *wake up*, Silvan. I did my best. Nobody else was looking out for you. And when finally you began to hear things, it wasn't me you listened to. No, it was the faithful talking to you through the glass, whispering their prayers and their problems and telling you what a brave boy you'd been, all those centuries ago when you laid down your life for your creed. It's not my fault you believed it."

My shaking hands rain waxy dust on the shining stones. "You think this trick is a kindness."

"Kindness? You know what they did to me in the Old Testament, Silvan? *Archangel Raphael did bind Azazel hand and foot and cast him into the darkness: and made an opening in the desert and cast him therein. And placed upon him rough and jagged rocks, and let him abide there forever, and covered his face that he may not see light*. For eyeshadow! For a few bits of jewellery! *'The whole earth has been corrupted through the works that were taught by Azazel: to him ascribe all sin'.*"

The kohl runs in dirty canyons down his cheeks.

"Rather harsh," I mumble. There are hardly any deserts left, now. I imagine him lying there, alone and entombed in clay, and feel an odd sort of kinship. Perhaps the commiseration shows on my face, because Az shrinks, losing the corpse paint, becoming once again dandified and candy-striped and pert.

"I felt sorry for you," he says, defeated. "Okay? And I wanted to fuck with you a bit. 'Cause you're cute and I'm bored and why not? And the world is going to Hell. Nothing you or I can do about it."

"I never really met Mister Lenin, did I?"

He lets a green tinge crawl across his face, but seems to tire. It vanishes. "No."

"And the men who robbed Valerius?"

"Guilty."

What lengths he has gone to.

"My Lenin skit was tip top, though, you must agree." He summons a ghost of his old jollity. "And you were adorable. So exceedingly patient with the grandiose little Rusky. That's you all over. Forgiving to a fault."

"And Shelter Girl? Was she you, too?"

"No. Or her stupid dream. Believe it or not."

Good. But... I hold my breath, such as it is. "And Venus?"

"What does it matter? I was on the stage, did I ever tell you? Pre-war Paris – the *Grand-Guignol*. When they invented the telephone, I did a sketch about a number you called to listen to a live murder on the other end. Oh, the things I'll show you in France. And then there's India, and Egypt..."

He is stalling. Dapper little gangster, for all his charms he hasn't a drop of the secret, golden light of Shelter Girl in her ragged denim. And he knows nothing of my faculty for silently drawing out secrets.

"Lenin was to take you down a peg," he admits. "And who better to jog your memory about the wax than Venus? She's real. And oblivious, if that matters. You made a friend. Three cheers for you." He looks at me side-on, under his hair, as if he can't bear to face me. "Come with me. When the rains take over. Wear the crown and let me love you and be free."

The clouds crack open over Florence. For all I know, he's arranged that, too, the kind of romantic scene one as old as me might unironically enjoy. I wonder where Shelter Girl is. Will she, like my beloved Bernadette, be hailed as a mystic and enshrined in Catholic lore? I had hoped better things for her. A dry home with her husband, and perhaps, if I indulge my imagination, the return of her muddy devotees and their pagan crusade to revive the Earth. People may strive for what they need, but they rarely get it. Think of those pitiable clownfish leaving their dying anemones. The Universe has long since ceased to speak to me of logic or of fairness. Or beauty. I have nothing left.

Az morosely regards the rushing waters of Cryptspace. "It's nearly dawn, Silvan. You need to go home. If you're gone in the morning, there'll be pandemonium."

"A bit of pandemonium now and then is good for the soul, I'd say."

We both turn. A woman, nude, red in the chest where her vital organs shine and spill. Venus.

"You can't come down here," Az says. "You're not dead."

"Not alive, though, was I, in the first place?"

He isn't used to being spoken to like that. One shoulder-twitch and he is magnificent again, a ten-foot sphinx of a being draped in garlands of African blood diamonds and the teeth of long-extinct sharks. You were wrong, painters of Cryptspace: Raphael, Botticelli, Leonardo... these creatures don't have wings. You were wrong, Delaroche. There are no haloes here. And though I draw back, awe-struck by Azazel's terrible beauty, Venus stands firm. She offers her hand and I hold it.

Azazel unhinges his jaw, and savagery comes seething out. "Don't take her hand. Don't you *dare* take her hand when you rejected mine. A box of bones, that's all you'd amount to without me. I offer you devotion without end. If you want me to love you, you'll do as I say."

Venus squeezes my hand. The crushed hull of a pleasure yacht comes barrelling down the stream towards us, and I have time to register 'The Jolly Jamaican', upside down in a cheery red font.

"Close your eyes."

"Why?"

She makes a face at me. "Have a little faith."

And she tips us both waterwards.

WAX, AS IT turns out, is a fantastic life preserver. We cling to the wreck of the yacht in the spinning waters of Cryptspace, sucked out at speed from the underground lanes of the dead and into the open living sea. As I watch the red tunnels fade into the watery fog, I hold fast to Venus' hand, letting the salty currents cascade through my hair. Huh, I think. Not my hair. Signor Sarti's. I suppose I ought to harbour the feelings of the jilted creation, a shade of Az's hurt and confusion, railing away at God and Sarti and the Roman guardians of Fate. But I'm really not that clever.

We surface somewhere without horizons. Venus has brought me to a rusty oilrig, long sucked dry, and she uses her waxy buoyancy to spring from the water and grab the rungs of a ladder.

"Come on," she shouts over her dripping shoulder. "There's no one here to stick us in a glass box."

Below us, where the water is clear, I see rooftops and sun loungers. With a wave of vertigo, I realise this is no oilrig and recognise – God only knows how, considering

– a helicopter landing pad glowing far below my feet. This was a lookout station, high upon the head of some long-dead billionaire's island villa. I see the wing of a downed airbus balancing on a third storey veranda, a dead leviathan waiting to be picked clean.

I am panting. I haven't seen the outside world like this, since… "Venus, dawn is coming. Cryptspace will close – he can't follow us. But how will we ever get back?"

"I didn't think too far ahead," she admits. "But look. Look there." Venus stretches out her arm, and I follow her pale finger to a shimmer of movement beneath the water's surface.

I see white and I see orange. In the wreck of the dead island, aquatic plants have sprouted, tumbling from mansion windows and creeping over tennis court skeletons. I do not know the name of this place, but neither do the clownfish. They swish in and out of the swaying vines as happily as if the icecaps had never melted at all. Not all lost. Not all doomed to run aground and freeze. Something loosens within me. Something shrugs off its bonds.

Venus is laughing. Not at the fish, though their endurance is a sight to make us both smile. No, she is looking at me, her long braid unravelled by seawater. She is laughing, and there's none of Aurelia's malice in it, not even the same old *how'd you get so handsome* giggle of the Catholic schoolgirls lining up to kiss the glass of my bower. Venus looks at me with what might be called pride.

"No sign of a break-in," she says. "Guards and vigils by every entrance, day and night… and yet, you've gone and pulled off the empty tomb trick. This is a miracle, Silvan. You've performed a real-life miracle."

A pale sun shyly rises. When morning comes, my devotees will find the altar at Saint Blaise's empty. My first dereliction of duty. It frightens me, but then I recollect what Thérèse said about God singling me out for the impossible. Even Az would admit that is precisely what I have done. Staring down at the clownfish shimmying about in their new home, I realise my visitors will make of my disappearance what they will. I know Shelter Girl shall, though I pray she makes something good of it, something hopeful. If my presence gave her strength, I only hope my absence serves to throw it into beautiful relief.

I have faith in her.

"This is the world. Look at it, Silvan. Look at the wide, wide world." Venus stares out at the fading stars and the faint coloured dots I imagine must be Johann's singing planets. "Signor Sarti never envisioned all this, I'll bet, when he made us both."

"I suppose this makes you my sister." I say it cautiously. I don't want to impose.

"In a roundabout way, it does."

She turns to me. Her pearls shine with salt water and the red cavern of her chest, familiar to me now, is somehow altered.

"Although…" she says, following my gaze. "Look at that. I've lost my heart."

ACKNOWLEDGEMENTS

I was fifteen when I stood over the incorrupt body of Saint Spyridon. It was my first visit to Corfu Town, a summer holiday with my parents. Peeking out onto a narrow street of lace-makers, icon sellers, and jewellers' shops, the modest exterior of Spyridon's shrine made its entrance easy to miss. There was certainly no fanfare for the miracle within as I stepped down into the perfumed candlelight. The Greek Orthodox Jesus possessed a strange allure; stern and penetrating, totally removed from the acoustic-guitar-and-custard-creams Sundays I spent in church at home. It's heretical to say it, but the shrine had magic.

I was baptised under the Moorish arches of Gibraltar's Cathedral of the Holy Trinity and raised in the considerably less colourful Church of England, back in Britain. It was all fairly strict, though my maternal grandmother, Stella, was a Catholic all but officially and a mystic at heart. Beneath her framed photograph of John Paul II and the silver crucifix he sent her in the seventies, her coffee table was laden with Spiritualist newsletters and books of psychedelic theories about Jesus' adventures in India. It was a peculiar mix of influences to grow up with, and it's little wonder I ended up wearing a pentagram whilst harbouring secret envy of all the fun I assumed the Catholics down the road were having, with their red lanterns and their Latin and their brave martyrs carrying eyeballs on plates. Protestants have bring-and-buy sales. I wanted blood.

So – fifteen and terribly earnest, despite the pentagram – I joined the queue to kiss the casket of Saint Spyridon: an eighteen-hundred-year-old bishop whose body, I was told, was preserved by a miracle of God. In the Church of England, you don't get many opportunities to kiss a dead man, and because Saint Spyridon was said to walk the streets at night, spreading his healing blessings, I knew my Nan, with her crystals and her dubious Chinese medicine, would approve. Yet as I joined the line disappearing into the dark chamber with its frescos of bearded, unsmiling patriarchs, I did my best to politely ignore my fellow pilgrims wiping their noses and clearing phlegm as they genuflected to press their lips against the cold silver. Would Saint Spyridon forgive me, I wondered, if I called it a day and slipped out to find a frappé? But there's no polite way to snub a saint, particularly when you're a Protestant, and the line grew rapidly shorter until I ended up inside a cave-like nook before a casket disappointingly hiding the miraculous body within. The metal was polished with kisses. I could hear behind me the *clack-clack-cough* of a woman thumbing olivewood prayer beads.

"Hello," I whispered, and left.

So, you see, I didn't get it out of my system when I had the chance.

Saint Silvan's remains lie in the Church of Saint Blaise, Dubrovnik. Over the years, I kept coming across this beautiful boy in online Fortean circles ("Top 10 Incorrupt Corpses!") but could never pin down any verifiable biographical details. There are several saints bearing variations of the name Silvan, and little is known about any of their lives. The status of his body is debatable enough. Depending who you ask, Silvan's bones are either stowed beneath the altar, encased inside a lovely wax model, or perfectly intact within his miraculous flesh. Whoever Silvan was or was not, his beauty continues to inspire awe from believers and non-believers all around the Earth. *Beauty Secrets* is, of course, fantastical fiction. But I liked the idea of Silvan having a voice.

Saint Valerius and Deodatus have been stunningly photographed by Paul Koudounaris in his book *Heavenly Bodies: Cult Treasures and Spectacular Saints from the Catacombs*. My Deodatus is the skull of an unknown individual, given a generic name by post-Reformation priests. After the rise of Protestantism in the 1500s, the Catholic Church went about restoring influence by removing unidentified skeletons from early Christian catacombs and canonising them as martyrs before shipping them off with new names to towns all over Europe. There, the bones would be dressed in jewels and adopted as the town's personal guardian. I'd love to know what the skeletons thought of it all.

There are many Anatomical Venuses still in existence, one of which I was lucky enough to see at The Museum of London's exhibition 'Doctors, Dissection, and Resurrection Men'. By replacing cadavers with something lifelike, the creators of the Venuses attempted to take the disturbing element out of biology, as well as solving practical problems, particularly the availability of bodies. We know that Signor Sarti invited women to view his Venus, so these waxworks were evidently considered sanitary enough for a more delicate audience. However, the combination of peepshow sensuality and exposed viscera still make for uncomfortable viewing. These naked girls are dead yet desirable, interlacing interestingly with the world of holy effigies where violent death is so often rendered with a veneer of ecstasy, even enjoyment.

My Venus is modelled on Clemente Susini's brunette wax Venus in Florence's La Specola Museum of Natural History. The poster Silvan reads whilst bending to pick up Venus' lipstick – *'Signor Sarti's celebrated Florentine Anatomical Venus'* – can be viewed in the Wellcome Collection's online image archive. There is no evidence Sarti made Silvan, if indeed you believe his body is a simulacrum.

I want to thank my first readers, Rachel and Thora, and a warm thanks to Gabriel, for making this novella possible.

FURTHER READING

Paul Koudounaris. *Heavenly Bodies: Cult Treasures and Spectacular Saints from the Catacombs*. Thames & Hudson, 2013.

Joan Carroll Cruz. *The Incorruptibles*: *A Study of the Incorruption of the Bodies of Various Catholic Saints and Beati*. TAN Books, 2010.

All The Saints You Should Know: allthesaintsyoushouldknow.com

Morbid Anatomy: morbidanatomy.blogspot.com

Wellcome Images: wellcomeimages.org

ABOUT THE AUTHOR

Verity Holloway writes speculative fiction and historical non-fiction. Born in Gibraltar in 1986, she holds an MA in Literature from Cambridge's Anglia Ruskin University, focusing on the poems of Dante Gabriel Rossetti. Her fiction is inspired by all things medical, historical, and religious, with a magical realist bent. In 2012, she published her first chapbook of poems, *Contraindications*. This is her first novella. Find her at verityholloway.com.